UP ALL NIGHT

UP ALL NIGHT

A SHORT STORY COLLECTION

★

Peter Abrahams

Libba Bray

David Levithan

Patricia McCormick

Sarah Weeks

Gene Luen Yang

★

With an introduction by
Laura Geringer

LAURA GERINGER BOOKS
HarperTeen
An imprint of HarperCollins*Publishers*

The excerpts on page vii are from *The Immense Journey* by Loren Eiseley, copyright 1946, 1950, 1951, 1953, 1955, 1956, 1957 by Loren Eiseley. Used by permission of Random House, Inc.

HarperTeen is an imprint of HarperCollins Publishers.

Up All Night: A Short Story Collection
Copyright © 2008 by HarperCollins Publishers

Introduction copyright © 2008 by Laura Geringer
"Phase Two" copyright © 2008 by Pas de Deux
"Not Just for Breakfast Anymore" copyright © 2008 by Martha E. Bray
"The Vulnerable Hours" copyright © 2008 by David Levithan
"Orange Alert" copyright © 2008 by Patricia McCormick
"Superman Is Dead" copyright © 2008 by Sarah Weeks
"The Motherless One" copyright © 2008 by Gene Luen Yang

Library of Congress Cataloging-in-Publication Data
Up all night : a short story collection / Peter Abrahams ; Libba Bray ; David Levithan . . . [et al.] ; with an introduction by Laura Geringer. — 1st ed.
        p.   cm.
    Summary: Six short stories about teens who stay up all night, written by award-winning authors.
    Contents: Phase 2 / by Peter Abrahams — Not just for breakfast anymore / by Libba Bray — The vulnerable hours / by David Levithan — Orange Alert / by Patricia McCormick — Superman is dead / by Sarah Weeks — The motherless one / by Gene Luen Yang.
    ISBN 978-0-06-137076-2 (trade bdg.)
    ISBN 978-0-06-137077-9 (lib. bdg.)
    1. Short stories, American. 2. Teenagers—Juvenile fiction. [1. Short stories. 2. Teenagers—Fiction. 3. Night—Fiction.] I. Abrahams, Peter, date. II. Bray, Libba. III. Levithan, David. IV. McCormick, Patricia, date. V. Weeks, Sarah. VI. Yang, Gene. VII. Bass, L. G. (Laura Geringer)
PZ5.U73 2008
[Fic]—dc22   2007021355
                                                                                   CIP
                                                                                    AC

Typography by Allison Limbacher
1 2 3 4 5 6 7 8 9 10
❖
First Edition

Introduction

Dear Reader,

When I was a teen, my favorite short stories often had to do with moments of wonder and amazement, when a single revelation transformed a character literally overnight. The tales were as varied as their tellers, but the theme that drew me was the same: Something kept the hero or heroine up all night; and at the end of the vigil that individual (for better or for worse) was never the same again.

In some cases a soul had been lost, in others found. Or innocence had been lost or perhaps regained. Or the power of speech had been sacrificed. Or a shift of perception had offered salvation when it was least expected. Always, something had irrevocably changed, between sunset and sunrise during the quiet hours when most mortals were fast asleep.

Those stories I loved—by Oscar Wilde, Edgar Allan Poe, Nathaniel Hawthorne, Hans Christian Andersen, Lafcadio Hearn, E.T.A. Hoffman, and Jacob and Wilhelm Grimm—linger still in my mind and heart. If you too tend to be nocturnal by nature, or even if you don't, I recommend them to you.

I also recommend to you one of the greatest of all insomniac writers, Loren Eiseley, whose essay "The

Judgement of the Birds" tells of his experience one night on the twentieth floor of a midtown hotel in New York City when, alone in the dark , he grew restless and on an impulse, opened the curtains: "I . . . peered out. It was the hour just before dawn, the hour when men sigh in their sleep, or, if awake, strive to focus their wavering eyesight upon a world emerging from the shadows. . . . The light was being reflected from the wings of pigeons who, in utter silence, were beginning to float outward upon the city. In and out . . . passed the white-winged birds on their mysterious errands. At this hour the city was theirs, and quietly, without the brush of a single wing tip against stone in that high, eerie place, they were taking over the spires of Manhattan. . . . As I crouched half asleep across the sill, I had a moment's illusion that the world had changed in the night, as in some immense snowfall. . . . To and fro went the white wings, to and fro. There were no sounds from any of them. They knew man was asleep and this light for a little while was theirs. Or perhaps I had only dreamed about man in this city of wings. . . . Perhaps I, myself, was one of these birds, dreaming. . . ."

Each of the stories in this collection presents in its own way what Loren Eiseley described so beautifully in that passage from *The Immense Journey*—a moment of vision from an inverted angle, a time when, by chance or intention, a human stood sleepless upon the border of two worlds at an hour when others were unconscious, and miraculously caught a brief transformative glimpse into the depths.

In Peter Abrahams's "Phase 2," a brush with the supernatural works in mysterious ways as an agent of change in the lives of two children who have lost their father. In Libba Bray's "Not Just for Breakfast Anymore," a rock concert evening of breathless misadventure and an underwater revelation bring unexpected rewards. In David Levithan's "The Vulnerable Hours," the simple question "What's up?" paves a winding road to a reciprocal moment between two lonely seekers of truth. In "Orange Alert," by Patricia McCormick, going too far cuts both ways in a sudden and highly satisfying reversal of power. In Sarah Weeks's "Superman Is Dead," the impact of the death of a pet, a divorce, the birth of a stepbrother, and an imagined murder come together in a loss of innocence that is all too poignantly real. In Gene Luen Yang's "The Motherless One," the age-old question "Why was I born?" becomes Monkey's quest and obsession, ironically causing the legendary character to ignore the signposts nature offers all around him and come dangerously close to losing the very life he is seeking to understand.

It gives me the greatest pleasure to have the masterful storytellers represented here gathered in one volume. Inspired by their narratives of a single night that matters, I invite you to write your own short story.

I hope you enjoy these unusual tales, as I have, and that whatever you select to take from them stays with you for many days and nights to come, waking and dreaming.

Laura Geringer
Publisher, Laura Geringer Books

STORIES THAT MAY KEEP YOU UP ALL NIGHT:
Isaac Asimov's "Nightfall"
Richard Connell's "The Most Dangerous Game"
Nathaniel Hawthorne's "Young Goodman Brown"
Ernest Hemingway's "A Clean, Well-Lighted Place"
James Joyce's "The Dead"
Guy de Maupassant's "Night: A Nightmare"
Edgar Allan Poe's "The Tell-Tale Heart"

Contents

PHASE 2

Peter Abrahams

Counting the hours," my dad wrote in his last email. "Exactly forty-six more and I'm out of this godforsaken place. Phase Two begins! Love you all." *All* meaning Mom, my eleven-year-old brother, Neddy, and me, Lara.

"Hey Mom," I said. "An email from Dad."

"Is everything all right?" Mom said, hurrying over from whatever she was doing, the laundry maybe—laundry, I remembered at that moment, that I'd promised to take care of before school. For some reason, Mom just couldn't get used to these emails coming in real time from a war zone, got alarmed whenever one turned up in the in-box. She leaned over my shoulder for a closer look at the screen, a bottle of spot remover in her hand. I was aware of her eyes tracking the words, could feel her concentration, so intense.

"What's the time difference again?" Mom said.

"Thirteen hours?" I said. "Or maybe with turning back the clocks it's—"

"Why can't you guys get this?" said Neddy, doing his homework at the kitchen table. He glanced at his watch. "It's eight thirty-five A.M. over there, A.M. tomorrow."

"That's good," said Mom.

"What is?" I said.

"That it's already tomorrow," Mom said.

"For God's sake," said Neddy. "Forty-six hours is forty-six hours." Probably the very words Dad would have said, but they wouldn't have sounded so annoying coming from him. Dad had a real gentle voice, deep but soft. Neddy's voice had a grating undertone even when he was in a good mood. But he and Dad both had that precise way about them, a precision you could see in Dad's email, how the grammar was always right and all the letters that should have been capitalized were. That precision was what made him such a great pilot. Nobody had told me that—I just knew. Once, when I was really little and we still lived on the base, Dad took me up in an old World War Two P-39, let me sit on his lap while he flew. Somehow his hands on the controls looked intelligent, as though each contained a tiny brain, thinking about every movement. I felt so safe, like the sky was my natural element. He even did a few barrel rolls, just to hear me laugh. Dad liked my laugh, for some reason. "Where'd Lara get a laugh like that?" he'd say.

★ ★ ★

Mom went to the calendar on the fridge door. "So forty-six hours from now means Thursday at six thirty-five P.M.?"

"Duh," said Neddy.

Mom took a red marker and made a big ! in Thursday's square. That didn't mean Dad was coming home on Thursday; they always flew to the Ramstein base in Germany first. But he'd be back by Sunday or Monday and then there'd be big changes, what Dad called Phase Two of our lives. Phase Two started with Dad resigning from the service and taking a piloting job with Executive Air, a charter company. Mom and Dad were real happy about it. He'd be home three or four nights a week and most weekends, and the pay was good. They'd already put down a deposit on a house in almost the nicest part of town. A house with a pool! Plus Neddy and I were going to have our own bedrooms for the first time, instead of sharing. Even the address sounded great: 88 Hickory Lane. I'd already written it on all my schoolbooks, scratching out "3712 Baseline Road, Apt. 19."

Mom went to the beauty parlor and had highlights put in her hair. Once or twice I heard her singing to herself. Mom had a beautiful singing voice, had even made a demo for some record producer when she was a teenager. She cleaned the apartment from top to bottom and rearranged the furniture. Thursday night she made a special dinner—pork roast with orange sauce and pecan pie for dessert. Mom kept glancing at the clock. At six thirty-five she went to the fridge and took out a bottle of wine. Mom didn't drink wine, didn't drink at all. "Who wants a little sip?" she said.

"Bring it on," said Neddy.

Mom gave him a look. "Just this once, buster," she said.

I took three glasses from the cupboard and set them on the table. Mom was unscrewing the cap off the wine when the buzzer went. She pressed the intercom button and said, "Yes?"

Then came some static, followed by a man's voice. "Mrs. Byron?"

"Yes?"

"First Lieutenant Kevin Skype and Chaplain Ferrarra to see you, ma'am. May we come up?"

Mom went white, the color of a corpse in the movies. The bottle of wine slipped from her hand and smashed on the floor, but while it was still in midair I noticed a soaring eagle on the label, rising in a pure blue sky, the image so clear. I remembered that eagle way better than anything that happened in the next few days.

There's a crazy thing I've thought about a lot of times and still don't understand. After someone dies—someone close to you, I mean, like a father— why should it be so important to get the body back and bury it? They're dead, right? That's the big thing. So what difference should it make? All I can tell you is that it does. It makes a big difference. I know, because we never got to bury my dad. Chaplain Ferrarra said there was nothing to recover after the crash, nothing human to bury. We had the funeral—packed church, trumpeter playing Taps, buddies of Dad's who called him a hero. They were all so gentle, big guys kind of trying to make themselves smaller, if you know what I mean, so they wouldn't be towering over the three of us. Something strange happened to me in the church: I suddenly felt so alive, more alive than I'd ever been, just glowing with it, hyperconscious of my beating heart, the blood flowing through my veins, the oxygen filling my lungs. That shamed me, but there was nothing I could do about it. Anyway, the full-of-life feeling didn't last long. Soon the three of us were back in Apartment 19 at 3712 Baseline Road and I was all hollowed out. Going through the motions: an everyday saying that I now understood through and through.

We got the $6,000 death gratuity from the Army in three days, and the next week Mom returned to work. We were going to be all right for money, she said.

"I'm sorry about 88 Hickory Lane," she said.

"Oh, Mom," I told her. "Don't even think about it." Neddy and I went back to school. At first everyone made a big effort to be nice to us. Then they slipped back to normal. Normal was better. From time to time, just for a moment or two, shooting hoops in P.E., say, I felt normal too. Not normal like before, back in Phase One, but a new kind of normal. Neddy, too—after a couple weeks, I even heard him laughing on the phone.

But Mom cried at night. She tried to muffle the sound, but the wall between the bedrooms was thin. And she wasn't eating. Her clothes started hanging loosely on her body, and when I hugged her good-bye in the mornings, I could feel all the ribs in her back. Then she got the idea that maybe Dad had survived the crash, was a prisoner somewhere in the desert, or injured and holed up in a cave. Neddy's face got all hopeful the first time she offered up this new theory.

"Mom?" I said. "You really think so?"

Her voice sharpened. "Why not? There's no body. And who's more resourceful than Dad?"

"Nobody, Mom, it's just . . ."

She wrote a letter to the Army, asking them to send out search parties. When no answer came after three or four days, she started calling. Chaplain Ferrarra came to the apartment again, this time with a major. The major had pictures of the crash site.

"Sure you want to see these, ma'am?" he said.

"Absolutely," said Mom. "Kids—go to your room."

Neddy and I shook our heads. Not that we wanted to see, exactly, more like we had to. Mom glared at us for a moment or two; then her look softened a little.

"All right," she said.

The major spread color photos on the kitchen table. We looked at blackened metal scraps twisted and scattered across a desert floor, not the beautiful kind of desert I'd come to know a little the two years we were posted to the base in Tucson, but just a stark and empty ugly nothing. Those scraps, so small and deformed, didn't add up to a plane or anything else.

The major's eyes were on Mom, just waiting patiently.

Mom met his gaze. "He could have bailed out," she said. "Maybe into those hills in the background."

"Problem is, ma'am," said the major, "there wasn't time. Surface-to-air missile—eyewitnesses saw the hit. Direct on the nose. The aircraft broke up in midair."

Mom's brow furrowed. I could see how hard she was thinking. "What if he saw it coming and hit the ejection button at the last second?" she said.

The major gazed at her and said nothing.

Mom pressed on. "He had great vision," she said. "Twenty-ten in his right eye."

The major shifted one of those horrible pictures around in case Mom wasn't seeing it properly.

"Ma'am," said the chaplain, very quiet. I noticed a tiny shaving cut under his chin, still seeping a drop or two of red.

★ ★ ★

Mom stopped calling the Army, wrote no more letters. But she still wasn't eating, and now, instead of crying in the night, she was up till all hours on the computer. Mom had never shown any interest in online things before.

"Mom?" I asked one morning. "What are you doing on the computer?"

"Research," she said, deep dark depressions under her eyes.

"Into what?"

"Just research."

That night she didn't come home till real late. I

was awake. In this new normality I didn't sleep quite as well as in the old one. She went into the bathroom, her footsteps quicker than they'd been for a while, like she wasn't dragging herself around. Water ran. Then I heard the squeak of her bedsprings. After that, silence. No crying.

"Lara?" said Neddy, very softly.

"Yeah?"

"You awake?"

"Yeah."

"I think I know where she's been."

"Where?"

"To a seense."

"Huh?"

"That's what she's been checking out online. I followed her tracks."

Not nice, but that didn't seem important right now. "What's a seense?" I said.

"You know," said Neddy. "Where you sit around the table in the dark and try to talk to spirits."

"Oh," I said. "A séance."

"That's how you pronounce it?"

"SAY-ahnse."

"Séance," Neddy said.

We lay in the darkness, not speaking. I closed my eyes but couldn't sleep. A siren sounded far away.

After a while Neddy spoke, even quieter than before. "Spirits means spirits of the dead, right?"

"Right."

★ ★ ★

Mom came back late the next night. And the next and the next and the next. Her footsteps slowed down. The muffled crying started up again. She missed a couple days' work—a Thursday and Friday—maybe not even calling in the second time, because her boss phoned and I heard Mom saying how sorry she was and that it would never happen again. That wasn't quite enough for her boss, because after listening for a few moments, she said, "Please give me one more chance." And then: "Thank you."

Mom stayed home that night. Saturday morning she was up early, already making waffles when Neddy and I went into the kitchen. She sat down at the table with us, rubbing her hands in an enthusiastic way; but all that darkness around her eyes was even worse than before.

"How are the waffles?" she said.

"Good, Mom," I said. "Thanks."

Neddy mumbled something, totally incomprehensible with his mouth full.

"Aren't you having any?" I said.

"I'm not hungry," Mom said. "I had a big dinner." Which wasn't true; she'd hardly touched her food last night. She spooned a little sugar into her coffee, took a sip. "I've met this interesting woman," she said.

"Yeah?" I said.

Neddy poured more syrup on his waffles, globs of it. Dad would have said, "Son?" And Neddy would have stopped. Mom didn't seem to notice.

"Her name's Mrs. Foxe," Mom said. "With an e. She's lived all over the world."

"An Army brat like us?" I said, although we really hadn't lived too many places—just here, Tucson, and San Diego.

"No, nothing like that," Mom said. "She's . . . different."

"How?" I said.

Mom stirred her coffee again, gazed into the tiny black whirlpool she'd made, spinning round and round, very fast. "There's more to life than just the everyday things," she said. "That's one of Mrs. Foxe's beliefs."

"More to life such as?" I said.

Mom's eyes met mine for a moment, looked away. "I'm talking about beyond the material world," she said.

"Outer space?" Neddy said, syrup dripping down his chin.

"Beyond outer space, too," Mom said.

"There's nothing beyond outer space," said Neddy. "It goes on and on. That's why they call it outer space."

"This isn't about space," Mom said. "Or science, or any of that. It's about . . ."

"About what, Mom?" I said.

"The spiritual world, I guess you'd say."

"You mean religion?" I said.

"Not exactly," said Mom. "What Mrs. Foxe says is that the life force is so strong, it leaves an undying imprint. Those are her exact words."

"An undying imprint where?" I said.

Mom gave me a long look. "That's the question."

"What is?" said Neddy.

"Where the undying imprints go," I told him.

"Undying imprints of what?" he said.

I turned to Mom.

"Of the living," she said. "After they're gone."

"So it is about space," Neddy said.

One of Mom's eyelids twitched; I'd never seen that happen to her before. "I don't understand," she said.

"You said these imprints or whatever go somewhere," Neddy explained. "All somewheres are in space." That last part could have been spoken by Dad, word for word. But it would have sounded nicer.

Mom rubbed her face; her skin looked tired, took a moment or two to resume its tautness.

"Mrs. Foxe says that these undying imprints go where souls go."

"Souls?" I said.

"Just another word for undying imprints," Mom said. "She says."

"Souls of the dead," I said.

Mom's voice was quiet. "The undying part." She stared into her coffee. "Mrs. Foxe believes . . . in fact, she has actually experienced . . . that under certain circumstances some extrasensitive people are able . . ." She went silent. I heard the bus going by down on the street; we were on the route for the number 7 bus, heading downtown. Mom looked up. "Do you kids know what a séance is?"

We nodded.

"Mrs. Foxe is one of those extrasensitive people," Mom said.

"You've been trying to communicate with . . . with Dad?" I said.

"Mrs. Foxe thinks we're very close to making contact," Mom said. "She can feel it. There's just one last roadblock in the way."

"What's that?" I said.

"The venue."

"Huh?" said Neddy.

"The place where we've been having the séances. She says here would be better. So . . ."

"So?"

"So we're going to try tonight. After midnight is best, when you kids are in bed anyway."

"No," I said.

"No?" said Mom.

"Us too," said Neddy.

"I don't . . ."

★ ★ ★

Mrs. Foxe smelled like flowers, lots of them. She had huge liquid eyes and a high forehead, very smooth although the part of her neck showing above the ruffled collar of her silk blouse looked wrinkled.

"What lovely children!" she said. She glanced around the kitchen, lit only by three big candles burning on the round table—red, white, and blue—took a deep breath of the air, full of the smell of burning incense, raised her hands slightly, and went still. "Yes," she said, holding the pose for a moment or two, "this will do. You've done well, Julie."

"Oh," said Mom. "Thanks."

"So if we'll just get the donation out of the way, we can start."

Mom went into the bedroom. Mrs. Foxe looked at Neddy, then at me. "I understand you'll be accompanying us on our journey," she said.

"Where to?" said Neddy.

Mrs. Foxe just smiled. Mom came back with her purse, took out her checkbook.

"Cash works so much better," said Mrs. Foxe.

Mom handed her some bills. I didn't see how much, but there were at least two twenties. Mrs. Foxe stuffed the money down the front of her blouse with a smooth quick movement, like one of those close-up magicians. Her hands were soft and plump, with crimson nails.

"The longest journey begins with a single step," she said.

None of us knew what to make of that.

"So let us take that step," said Mrs. Foxe. "Time and tide et cetera. Places, everybody."

We all moved toward our regular chairs.

"Whoa!" said Mrs. Foxe.

We froze. The candlelight gleamed in her eyes. "Where does *he* sit?"

Mom rocked back a little. "Where he used to—?"

"His chair, dear," said Mrs. Foxe.

Mom pointed to Dad's chair.

"That chair stays empty," said Mrs. Foxe. "I will sit here, the children there and there, and Julie like so. And in front of *his* place, we require something personal."

"Something personal?" Mom said.

"Something he used when he walked on this side," said Mrs. Foxe. "It needn't be important—in fact, a little everyday object is often best, especially if a deport is in the offing."

"A deport?" said Mom.

"I'll explain later," said Mrs. Foxe, glancing at her watch.

Mom hadn't gotten around to packing up Dad's

things, although she'd started once or twice. She left the room, returned with a baseball trophy, a framed letter from the secretary of defense, Dad's laptop, and a safety razor.

"Ah, perfect," said Mrs. Foxe, selecting the razor and setting it on the table in front of the empty chair. "Now we may sit."

Mom put the trophy, letter, and laptop on the sideboard and we sat, Mrs. Foxe removing her embroidered coat and hanging it on the back of her chair. She gazed at the white candle. It made a low sizzling noise.

"The travelers will hold hands," she said.

That had to mean us. I held hands with Mrs. Foxe and with Mom, just able to reach her across Dad's empty place; and Neddy did the same. Mrs. Foxe's hand was warm, Mom's icy cold. Mrs. Foxe's eyes closed. For some reason, so did mine. It got very quiet.

"Breathe," said Mrs. Foxe. She took in a deep breath, slowly let it out. "Breathe as one." We took in deep breaths, let them out slow, breathing as one.

"Now," said Mrs. Foxe, "let each of us picture in our minds the strongest, clearest image of . . . of . . ."

"Richard," said Mom.

"Right," said Mrs. Foxe. "The strongest, clearest image of Richard-slash-Dad that we can."

I tried to see Dad in my mind and drew a complete blank. Mom, Neddy, my teachers and friends—I could picture them all without effort, but not Dad. I opened my eyes. Everyone else's eyes were closed. Mrs. Foxe spoke, her voice now soft but very deep. "We haven't lost you, Richard. We know where you are."

I could feel the pulse strengthen in Mom's hand. And her skin seemed to be growing warmer.

"Are we all now projecting a strong mental image?" said Mrs. Foxe. "A mental image powerful enough to reach the beloved?"

"Yes," said Mom, eyes closed tight, voice trance-like.

"Kind of," said Neddy.

I gazed at that razor, and suddenly a vision of Dad shaving swam into my mind, a clear vision of him tilting up his chin to get at the stubble underneath. Was it powerful? I don't know, but I felt chills. "Yes," I said, and closed my eyes.

"Richard," said Mrs. Foxe. "Four faithful travelers are trying with all their power to reach you. If you can hear us, or see us, or sense us, please give a sign."

In my mind, the image of Dad shaving under his chin began to fade, replaced by nothing. One of the candles sizzled again. Could that be a sign? I took a peek. The flame of the white candle wavered; the others were still, burning straight up.

"Look," I said.

Everyone opened their eyes. Mrs. Foxe saw what was happening. She turned to me and smiled a little smile. "Hush, child—haste is the enemy," she said. Now her hand felt positively hot.

"But is it a sign?" I said. "The candle flickering like that?"

Mrs. Foxe didn't answer. We watched the flame. All at once it stopped wavering, stood straight like the others.

Mrs. Foxe sucked in her breath. "I can feel your presence, Richard," she said. "Very near." She leaned forward slightly. "Give us a sign, we beg you."

I felt prickles on the back of my neck. Mom's eyes were huge and dark, her face tilted up, like a figure in an old religious painting. Neddy's eyes, on the other hand, were narrow, almost as though—

The razor wobbled.

Beyond a shadow of a doubt. No way to miss that movement—the razor lay all by itself on the table, gleaming in a circle of candlelight. It had wobbled. But even though there was no doubt, I began to doubt almost right away. At that precise moment, the moment of reawakening doubt, the razor wobbled again, and then, as though to crush any doubt for all time, it shifted, sliding a good two inches across the table and then rotating in a full circle.

"Oh my God," Mom said. "Richard." A tear spilled out of each dark eye, slid slowly down her cheeks, leaving golden tracks.

"Welcome to the circle, Richard," said Mrs. Foxe. She paused, almost as if to allow time for Dad to say something polite in return. Then she said, "Have you anything to tell us?"

Silence. The razor lay on the table, motionless now. The flame of the white candle burned straight, unwavering.

"Do you have a message for your family?" Mrs. Foxe said. "Are you happy? Are there any wishes you'd like to—"

Suddenly Mrs. Foxe's right shoulder sagged, as though someone behind her had leaned on it, someone with a heavy hand. Mrs. Foxe glanced behind her, looked a bit pained. "Oh, dear," she said. "I'm afraid you don't know your own strength."

Mom rose, slowly, as though pulled by some force, her eyes on the shadows behind Mrs. Foxe. "Oh, Rich," she said, tears flowing freely now, "I miss you so much."

"Julie?" said Mrs. Foxe, straightening up and maybe a bit alarmed. "Really much better form to remain seated. We can't always predict—"

But Mom didn't hear. She was moving around the table, toward whatever stood behind Mrs. Foxe. "Did it hurt, Rich?" she said. "I hope it didn't hurt.

You're not hurting now, are you?" Mom reached the space behind Mrs. Foxe, raised her arms, encircled them around what appeared to be nothing, hugged my invisible dad. "I love you, Rich," Mom said. Her voice sounded calm, as calm as I'd ever heard it, serene. "I loved you from the moment I laid eyes on you, and I always will." She wasn't crying anymore, just stood there, gently rubbing a back no one could see.

But I was crying. "Can you feel him, Mom?" I said.

Mom nodded to me, the way you'd nod over someone's shoulder. I rose. Was that Neddy getting up too? I wanted to touch Dad, so much. But Mrs. Foxe grabbed my arm—she turned out to be very strong—and sat me back down. Then she got up, took Mom's arm more gently, and said, "Best not to pressure visitors from the spirit world too much, at least not at first. Wouldn't want to scare them off, would we?"

"Oh, no," said Mom. She let Mrs. Foxe lead her back to her seat.

We sat around the table. The air tingled now. I felt

Dad's presence, no question.

"Thank you, Richard," said Mrs. Foxe. "We thank you for appearing among us. I sense you are fading now, and hope you will see fit to come again."

"He's not fading," Mom said. "I don't sense him fading."

"Perhaps not," said Mrs. Foxe. "But we don't want to demand too much the very first—"

The flame of the white candle wavered and then rose straight again.

"Richard?" said Mrs. Foxe. "Richard?"

The room was silent. The silence went on and on. Mom watched the white candle, burning in an ordinary way now, like the other two. I stopped sensing Dad's presence.

Mrs. Foxe pushed back her chair. "Well," she said. "For a first attempt, quite successful, *n'est-ce pas?*"

"Maybe it's not over," Mom said. "Let's give him a chance to—"

"It's over," said Mrs. Foxe. She pointed to the table. The razor was gone.

Mom gasped. So did I. Neddy? Maybe not.

"A deport, my dear," said Mrs. Foxe. "An object borne away into the spirit world." She got up, flicked a switch, turning on the overhead light.

Mom rose too, blinking in light that now seemed much too harsh. "When can we do it again?"

"Soon, if you like," said Mrs. Foxe, donning her embroidered coat. "You've got my cell?"

★ ★ ★

Mrs. Foxe left. Mom turned from the door, wrapped me and Neddy in her arms, held us for a long, long time. No one said anything. We were all wiped out from emotion.

After a while, Mom said, "Let's get some sleep." She went into her bedroom. Neddy and I went into ours. I sank down on my bed. Neddy walked over to his and punched his pillow, real hard.

"Huh?" I said.

He turned, came closer, spoke in a low, angry voice, his face all red. "She's a fake."

"Mrs. Foxe?" I said. "What the hell are you—"

Neddy reached into his pocket and took out the razor. He held it on the palm of his hand. I actually had to touch it to make sure it was real.

"You took it off the table?" I said. "I don't understand."

"*She* took it off the table," Neddy said. "Remember when she got Mom to sit back down?"

"Yeah."

"She scooped up the razor at the same time, without even looking, real smooth, and dropped it in the pocket of that coat of hers."

"Oh my God. Are you sure?"

"Course I'm sure," said Neddy. "I took it out the next second, while her back was turned. And you know what else?"

"What?"

"The way it moved on the table, spinning around and all that?"

"Oh no."

"Oh yeah. She had a magnet between her knees, under the table. I peeked. She didn't see me—her eyes were on Mom the whole time."

I felt sick. "What about the flame?"

"She has this real sneaky way of blowing out through her nose," Neddy said.

"So none of it was real?"

Neddy shook his head. He looked like he was about to start crying, and Neddy wasn't a crier.

"But I felt him there," I said. I wasn't a crier either, but I was crying now. Then I got angry, real angry, and the crying stopped. I wiped my face on my sleeve, pulled myself together. "This is bad," I said.

"What are we going to do?" said Neddy. "Tell Mom?"

I thought about that, picturing how Mom had hugged empty space and told Dad how she'd always loved him. Dropping the truth on her? No way. But Mrs. Foxe would be back, again and again, getting her hooks deeper and deeper into Mom, taking every cent we had.

"What happens when she discovers she doesn't have the razor?" I said.

"She'll just figure it fell out, getting into her car or something like that," Neddy said. "A little thing like that won't stop her."

He was right. But how could we let this go on? Over on the desk, the green button on the computer we shared was blinking slowly in sleep mode. That reminded me of the four objects, one in particular. I went over to the computer and woke it up. I wasn't a great computer person, but Neddy was.

"Got an idea," I said.

Neddy came closer. "Using our Wi-Fi?" he said.

"Yeah," I said. We were turning out to be a team. Neddy sat in front of the computer, started tapping away. He figured everything out real fast, was almost done when we heard a sound from the kitchen, maybe a chair scraping on the floor. I opened the bedroom door, went to look.

Mom was at the table, standing behind Dad's empty chair. She wore a nightgown now, and her hair was kind of wild. The candles were burning again, the only light in the room. Mom was facing in my direction, but she didn't seem to see me.

"Mom?"

She jumped, startled. "Lara? What are you doing up?"

"I couldn't sleep."

"Me either," Mom said. She put a hand on Dad's chair. "I've been kicking myself."

"Why?" Had she figured out that Mrs. Foxe was a fraud, problem solved?

Far from it. "There was so much more I wanted to say to Dad," Mom said. "And *he* never really got a chance to say anything."

"What do you mean?"

"They speak sometimes, these . . . these souls. Mrs. Foxe has seen it happen. I'm going to call her first thing in the morning, get her to come back tomorrow night." Mom bit her lip. "What if she's booked?"

I heard our bedroom door open, glanced over, saw Neddy in the doorway. Things were moving faster than we'd anticipated, but why not? I raised my eyebrows. He gave a little nod.

"Mom?" I said. "Why don't we try right now?"

"Oh, I don't think Mrs. Foxe would come over now."

"Without her, Mom."

"Without Mrs. Foxe? That won't work."

"Why not?" I said. "We know how it goes."

"It's worth a try," Neddy said, coming toward the table.

"Well . . ." said Mom. "I guess it can't hurt. Can it?"

"No, Mom."

I sat in my chair. Slowly Mom sat down in hers; there was still something trancelike about her movements.

"What object should we use?" I said.

"How about the laptop?" said Neddy, and before anyone could answer, he took Dad's laptop off the side table, opened it, and laid it between the candles.

"Start us off, Mom," I said.

"I'm not sure . . ."

"You know," said Neddy. "Breathe together, hold hands, and project a strong mental image."

"Oh, right," said Mom.

We breathed together, held hands, closed our eyes. Crazily enough, even though the fix was in and this time Neddy and I were the fixers, a hyper-clear image of Dad arose in my mind at once. He was out in the desert where the winds blew strong, back in the Tucson days, flying a box kite. Dad loved flying kites, built his own. I remembered this one very well: a strange-looking thing in the shape of a flying horse, but it had soared way, way up there. Dad had this enchanted expression on his face, like a little kid.

"I have an image," Mom said, so quietly I almost couldn't hear. "What comes next?"

"Travelers," Neddy said. "Three faithful travelers."

"Three faithful travelers are trying to reach you," Mom said. "Your wife and your beautiful children. If . . ."

"You can hear us, or see us," Neddy said.

"Or sense us," I said. "Please give a sign."

We sat in silence, eyes closed. Time passed. I started to wonder whether Neddy had messed up somehow, snuck a glance at him. His eyes were closed. He looked calm, and more than that, a lot like Dad in the box-kite memory.

"Please, Rich," Mom said. "There's so much I

want to say. I beg you." She sounded desperate, unbearably so. And at that moment, Dad's laptop made one of those beeps that signal a computer coming to life.

We all opened our eyes, gazed at the screen. It remained blank for a moment, and then a message popped up.

> Dear Family,
> I just want to tell you that I am fine. There is no pain and I love you very much and will always be with you. But the best thing you can do for me now is to go on with your lives and be happy. That can only happen if you dont contact me anymore. We will be together soon enough.
> Love,
> Rich/Dad

Neddy had left out the apostrophe in *don't*. Dad would never make a mistake like that. But Mom didn't seem to notice. She gazed at the screen, tears streaming down her face, not making a sound. I felt bad.

After a while, her tears dried up. She turned to us. "Dad's right," she said.

"Yes," we said.

"Can you print that for me, Neddy?"

Neddy rose, brought back the portable printer, printed the message. A few seconds later, the screen went blank. Mom kissed her fingers, touched the screen. Then she gave herself a little shake, almost like a dog, and blew out the candles. She didn't seem so trancelike now.

Faint milky light came through the window. The first number 7 bus of the day rumbled by. The air in the kitchen wasn't tingling anymore; we were back to a kind of normal.

Mom yawned, checked the time. "Oh my goodness," she said. "I don't want to see either of you till noon, at the earliest."

"Night, Mom."

"Night." She kissed us both and went to bed, taking the printout. We heard her sigh softly as she lay down, not an unhappy sigh, more like the kind of sigh when something is over. Almost at once, her

37

breathing grew slow and rhythmic, the breathing of sleep. We closed her door.

Neddy and I went into our bedroom, closed our own door. I'd never been so tired in my life.

"Good job," I said.

"You, too," said Neddy. "Do you—"

Our computer beeped, all on its own. We went over to the desk. Words appeared on the screen, but not in the usual way, more like they were materializing.

Thanks, kids. Good advice—not just for your mom, but for you, too.

I turned to Neddy. "Did you do this?" But all those commas in the right places—no way.

Neddy shook his head, eyes wide. Very slowly, almost a pixel at a time, the message dematerialized from the screen, leaving it blank. The air tingled.

DAN CUTRONA

Peter Abrahams is the *New York Times* bestselling author of the Echo Falls Mystery series, which includes *Behind the Curtain*, *Into the Dark*, and *Down the Rabbit Hole*, which won the Agatha Award and was an Edgar Award nominee. He's written numerous novels for adults, including *Delusion*, *Nerve Damage*, *End of Story*, *Oblivion*, *The Tutor*, *The Fan*, and *Lights Out*, which was an Edgar Award nominee as well. Peter has also written *Quacky Baseball*, a picture book with art by Frank Morrison. He lives in Massachusetts with his wife and four children. You can visit him online at www.peterabrahams.com.

NOT JUST FOR BREAKFAST ANYMORE

Libba Bray

Dallas traffic is a bitch, a bear, a hockey mask–wearing serial-killer-in-the-basement kind of scary, and Maggie is sure they are all going to die, die, die in a fiery crash. They will die on their way to the concert, and, worse, they will then be memorialized in the 1980 Crocker High School yearbook with pictures of roses drawn by the stoner AV students. There will be a bad poem about the most beautiful flowers meeting an early frost. The poem will *rhyme*, for Chrissakes. Maggie would rather have her entrails pulled through her nose than have that happen. She'd rather repeat "Devil Dog" Devalier's business typing class or accept a date with Jimmy Johnson, who she personally witnessed eating one of his boogers while he was stopped at a red light near the Whataburger on College Drive.

"Get over! Get over!" she screams to Diana, who's at the wheel.

Diana careens into the right lane without checking her side mirror. They narrowly miss a black Datsun, whose driver scolds them with a sharp blast of his horn.

"Holy shit!" Holly squeals from the backseat, laughing. She waves to the guy in apology.

Holly's waves get them out of a lot. She is the prettiest of them—tall and willowy, with long, shiny brown hair and Disney-animal brown eyes. Last summer she took a modeling course at the Barbizon School, a fact she likes to mention anytime she can.

The green-and-white exit marker looms up ahead. Maggie nudges Diana. "There's Twenty-one B!"

"We're gonna miss it," Justine pipes up from the

backseat, a mascara wand in one hand, a compact in the other.

"Hold on." Diana flies across the right lane, taking the exit ramp at such a clip that the girls bounce in their seats.

"Shit," Justine says. "You made me drop my mascara."

★ ★ ★

Maggie has gotten a special dispensation to come to Dallas for the Cheap Trick concert. Her mother has issued the following rules: 1) The girls will leave right after school before rush-hour traffic gets bad. 2) They will not smoke marijuana cigarettes, as her mother calls them. 3) If they get into trouble, Maggie can always call her dad, who lives in Dallas now. She gives Maggie a dime for just such an emergency phone call, and Maggie takes it, though she knows she will not use it.

"Holy shit, I thought we were gonna be that truck's hood ornament for sure," Justine says, wiping off her mascara wand with a McDonald's napkin she finds in the backseat. Justine never goes anywhere without eye makeup. Not even to the pool. She lines the insides of her lids with blue eyeliner and wears three coats of mascara because she read somewhere that this will make the whites of her eyes "pop," whatever that means.

"Keep a lookout," Diana says, and they fall into positions: Maggie and Holly scanning the right side of the road, Diana and Justine the left.

"See one. Over there," Justine calls.

Diana pulls into the gravelly parking lot of the Bullseye Liquor Corral and parks off to the side by the banged-up ice cooler, and they wait for somebody they can sweet-talk or bribe into buying booze for them.

"There's somebody." Justine points to a guy getting out of a white Ford pickup. He wears a cowboy hat and a large belt buckle in the shape of Texas.

Diana shakes her head. "Looks like a state trooper."

Maggie knows they have to pick carefully. The wrong guy—and it has to be a guy—could be an off-duty cop or a holy roller coming to drop off pamphlets for a church. At the very least, he could lecture them about underage drinking; at the worst, he could turn them in. They let two more cars pass—an old lady with orange lipstick and crazy penciled-in eyebrows, and two tattooed guys on Harleys whom Holly deems "too skeevy" to ask. Ten minutes pass without another car in sight.

"We'll be here all night," Justine laments.

The girl tribunal meets. It is decided that Diana will get the liquor. She's blond with big boobs and can usually pass for eighteen. Maggie will ride shotgun, sergeant at arms. Maggie hates this position. She gets nervous in liquor stores.

Diana and Maggie push through the doors into a dark hole of cool air. Bottles line the shelves like an alcoholic's dream library. The pimply-faced guy behind the counter looks up from his car magazine.

"Can I he'p you?" he asks. He's got a thick plug of chewing tobacco wedged next to his bottom lip. He spits a thin brown stream of it into a Dixie cup.

"Um, I hope so!" Diana flashes her brightest TV hostess smile, and the guy smiles back, which is a good start. She puts her hands on the counter and pushes her arms into her sides, which makes her boobs press together in a magnificent display of cleavage that does not go unnoticed by Chaw Boy. "Do you have peppermint schnapps?"

This is the part where Maggie gets nervous—will he ask for ID? She pretends to be very interested in the rack of free newsprint magazines that advertise homes for sale in the area. She leafs through one, letting her eyes scan over the ranch houses, the 4BD/2BA homes with mature trees. She sees a place for sale on Briarwood Street, which is her old street, the one where she used to live before her parents divorced last year, before her father came to live in Dallas.

Diana comes up behind her and grabs her by the arm. "Got it."

In the car, Diana pulls the bottle out of its brown paper bag, and they pass it around taking celebratory shots. The schnapps looks like water but it feels thick and hot as it burns down Maggie's throat, and she can't wait for it to do its neat party trick—the one where she feels numb enough to forget herself and be someone else for a while, someone fun and pretty and fearless. Her mother would be disappointed that she's drinking. Her mother is never pissed off, only "disappointed" and "concerned" and sometimes, if she's really angry, "a little upset."

"And your brother's sure the band's staying at the Hyatt?" Justine asks. She passes the bottle to Holly.

"That's what he said." Maggie's mouth tastes of oily peppermint.

"How does he know?" Diana asks.

"He heard it from this roadie they've used before," Maggie says, hoping this settles it.

Justine nods, grins. "I can't wait to see Cassie's and Maureen's faces when we tell them we partied with the band. Robin Zander's so sexy. Do you think he has a girlfriend?"

"Where's David now?" Holly asks. She's always had a thing for Maggie's brother.

"Houston, I think. Or maybe New Orleans." She

takes another sip, waiting for the bliss moment. "No. Houston."

David's been gone for six months. He graduated early and went on the road running lights and mixing sound for a Dallas bar band, Tower of Granite, that everyone says could be the next AC/DC, but Maggie thinks they're kind of lame. The lead singer likes to twirl the microphone on its wire, as if Roger Daltrey didn't practically trademark that move. Plus he refers to all groupies as "filling stations," which is just too gross for words.

Maggie and David speak in TV commercials. Not real ones but commercials they'd like to see on TV for products that should exist.

"Sugarlicious gum, because dentists have mortgages, too."

"For a religious dining experience, resurrect yourself and cross on over to Cheesus Crust Pizza!"

"The Tolkien Laundry Eraser: It's Lord of the Rings Around the Collar."

"Pervert's Photo-Mat. Take off your clothes, and we'll see what develops."

Back when Maggie's dad used to live with them, he would try to play along sometimes, but he was absolutely hopeless at it.

"Say *olé* to chicken mole!" he'd said once, holding up a plate of enchiladas.

"Dad, that is just pathetic," Maggie said, rolling her eyes. It was their regular Thursday night out when it was just the two of them. On Thursdays, Maggie's mom had night class and David was busy with his band.

"It rhymes," her dad protested. "What more do you want from your old man?"

Maggie put a hand to her heart in mock sympathy. "It's hard getting old, isn't it? I want you to know that when it's time and you've become a total embarrassment to us, I'm going to put you in the best home."

Her dad cocked an eyebrow. "I'll bet it'll be like *The Snake Pit* with Olivia de Havilland."

"She overacts," Maggie said through a mouthful of melted cheese. "I like Joan Fontaine better."

"Blasphemy," he said.

Maggie enjoyed these nights with her dad. Sometimes they went to the mall or to a museum, or they went to dinner at their favorite chain restaurant, Viva Zapata!, and pretended it was a special occasion so that the mariachi band would play at their table and they could wear oversized sombreros and shout out, *"Arriba!"* on cue. Other times they would stay up to watch an old movie where the people looked impossibly glamorous, and Maggie would put her head on her dad's shoulder and fall asleep. She'd usually open her eyes again about the time the credits rolled. Her mom would be snoring lightly in the armchair, and David would be sitting on the floor, eating ice cream and calling attention to Maggie's drool-encrusted shirt.

"Friend, is nighttime drooling a problem? Then say hello to the Saliva Suction Cup!"

She misses David and wishes he weren't so far away. But for now, she has the girls—Diana, Justine, and Holly. No one can remember exactly how or when it came to be this way; Holly and Maggie lived on the same street; Diana and Justine had been friends since fifth grade. But for more than a year now, it's been the four of them. They are rarely without one another. Especially on hot days, when they slather their skin in baby oil and iodine and lounge around the Holiday Inn pool on plastic chaises. The thick mauve-and-white strips on the chairs feel good supporting Maggie's stomach, like giant fingers. Maggie loves the feeling of the sun baking her slippery skin into something sticky, loves watching the pink blobs of iodine float through the Johnson's baby oil bottle like a home-made lava lamp.

After exactly forty-five minutes on her stomach, she flips onto her back and stares at the pool through half-mast eyes hidden behind big black sunglasses. Feigning sleep, she watches the guys roughhousing in the deep end, calling each other "asshole." She wonders if any of them think she's pretty or if there's only one kind of universal pretty, like Holly, or like Jaida Jordan, who made drill team captain two years in a row. Sometimes, as she studies the guys, bodies slick with pool water, shorts so heavy-wet they expose a small bit of butt crack, a mysterious trail of fine hair below the navel, she wonders if any of them are gay.

The first homosexual Maggie ever knew about was Christopher Jensen, who taught her Intermediate Jazz Dance class. Christopher was thin and blond with a high, feminine voice. Behind his back, the older girls liked to call him "ChriTHtopher," emphasizing a lisp that wasn't there. Maggie had been only eleven and hadn't understood. A girl named DeeDee, who went on to become homecoming queen and then a Dallas Cowboys cheerleader after that, said, "He's a little happy." She put "happy" in quotation marks. When Maggie still didn't get it, DeeDee leaned close and put her hand next to Maggie's ear, making Maggie feel suddenly anointed, the ecstasy of being chosen to share a secret with one of the big girls.

"He's a homo," DeeDee said, her whisper tickling down Maggie's neck like a kiss.

Christopher had come back into the room then, clapping his hands and asking to see his "Jazz

Babies" in position, and Maggie saw him as a completely different person. How could she not have noticed before? It was like looking at one of those optical illusion pictures where at first all you can see is a bunch of curvy lines and color, and then, suddenly, you see the hidden object—a lady's face in profile, a penguin with a hat—and from then on you always see it that way.

The day Maggie's parents split up was a cold one in January. Maggie was in her room stretching out for a run with David when their father knocked lightly on her door.

"Your mother and I want to talk to you," he said.

She followed him to the living room, down the long hallway with its careful, symmetrical placement of framed family photographs—baby pictures, a posed family photo at Yosemite that her brother had ruined (according to her mom) by making a "crazy person face"; wedding pictures of her grandparents; her own parents on their wedding day looking young and stiff and slightly terrified, seeming somehow less substantial than the cake; Maggie in a hobo costume for Halloween, a greedy bloodlust on her pudgy face; her brother in his Boy Scout uniform beside a volcano made of mud and baking soda, a red ribbon pinned to it. It was funny how sometimes the pictures made Maggie feel watched over and connected, like she could point to them and say, This is where I come from, these are my people. Other times, she would stand in the cool dark of that hallway really looking at the faces in the photographs and see total strangers; and then she would be startled by the very idea that she was tied to this place, this family, this shared history, with no say in the matter whatsoever.

In the living room, her mother was sitting on the brown plaid sofa under a framed poster of "Desiderata," a box of Kleenex beside her, her hand pressed to her mouth.

"Okay, we're here," David said. He pulled his leg up behind him in a quad stretch.

There were a lot of words that followed: *Things happen. Can't be helped. No one's blaming anyone here. Divorce.* Maggie felt as if she were sitting on the bottom of a pool watching the wavy forms of people above, hearing the muffled blah-blah of talk that she couldn't really decipher. She was safely away from it for as long as she could hold her breath.

"People can't change what they are," her dad said. His eyes were red. Her mom cried silently into a tissue. A burning sensation started in Maggie's chest, a need for air.

"I'm a homosexual," her dad said, and Maggie felt as if she had stayed too long on the bottom, and her lungs had filled with water.

After they hugged and someone made a joke, which they all laughed too hard at, and her mom asked if they'd want pancakes when they got back, Maggie and David went out for their run. He set the pace, a quick one, and the houses flew past in a numbing blur of ranch-colonial-faux Tudor.

When they reached the turnoff at the neighborhood clubhouse, David broke the silence. "What do you think about Daddy? Weird, huh?"

"Yeah," Maggie said. "Weird."

"I always kind of knew. Didn't you?"

"No. I had no idea."

She waited for him to say something then. *Oh, you poor, poor bunny rabbit. It's okay. Not everything is a lie. You and me, kid, we're gonna blow this one-horse gin stand and make electric wigwams till we're rolling in butter-crunch ice cream.*

"Homos," he said, picking up his feet, making her catch him. "They're not just for breakfast anymore."

★ ★ ★

It's nine o'clock, and Reunion Arena is packed for the sold-out show. Fans scramble to get their last-minute sodas and concert merchandise before Cheap Trick starts their set. The girls have skipped the opening act, which is some new wave group out of Boston that they don't care about. Their seats are in the top balcony, the nosebleed section as her dad calls it, but it was all they could afford.

"God, we'll never see anything from up here," Holly says, squinting at the stage way down below.

"Who cares? We're gonna meet them at the hotel, right, Mags?" Diana leans over to low-five Maggie.

Onstage, several roadies do a sound check. Every time they say, "Check, check" into the microphones, the crowd cheers for them. It's the kind of thing her brother has to do for Tower of Granite, and she hopes he's right about Cheap Trick being at the Hyatt. He seemed a little out of it last time they talked. He has a new girlfriend, Tanya, and he calls home less and less these days. One time Maggie left a message for him with Tanya, and she wasn't sure if he got it, because he didn't call back for two days. When she mentioned it to him, he just said, "Yeah, well, that's life on the road, babe."

A guy headed up the stairs stops at Maggie's seat.

"Hey, you wanna come sit with me? There's an empty seat," he says. He's cute, with a great smile and long, dark hair.

"No thanks," Maggie says.

The guy whistles. "Cold, man, cold," he says, and goes up to sit with his friends.

"Oh my god, that guy totally liked you—and

he's cute!" Justine says. "What's your problem?"

Maggie shrugs. "Not my type."

"What? Cute?"

"He looks like one of those guys you can't trust," Maggie says.

Justine laughs. "You're weird."

Maggie wants to shake Justine hard. She wants to tell her that you can't take everything at face value. People are like mirages, and from a distance they seem to be one thing, a cool spring, a date tree, a comfort zone. But when you get up close, they can turn out to be something you weren't expecting at all. And it's not like you can make them turn back into the mirage. You can't say, "Please go back to being a date tree. I was used to the date tree."

The lights dim and the crowd roars. It hurts Maggie's ears, but she's on her feet anyway; they all are. The band takes the stage. From where Maggie and her friends stand, the rock stars look like small, shiny puppets. They break into their opening number, and the girls scream and dance in the row.

"I can't believe we're gonna meet these guys

later!" Holly shrieks, and Maggie feels good that she's going to make that happen. She throws her arms around Holly's shoulders and they bump hips, singing along with Robin Zander's fierce growl, *"Would ya like to do a number with me? Would ya like to? Would you like to? Would you like to do a number with me?"*

For a moment, Maggie forgets everything. The music carries her along and she lets it, floating easily on the surface of her excitement and expectation.

An hour and a half into the concert, Maggie starts to feel funny. It's hot, and the pot smoke, sickly sweet and choking, is heavy in the air. Maggie feels like she's drowning. She needs air. She needs out.

She stumbles down the row toward the exit, not bothering to say excuse me to anyone. Diana's shouting something to her, but Maggie can't hear it over the band. It's like every sound is coming to her through waves of choppy ocean. She staggers into the bright hallway. The lights hurt her eyes after so much time in the dark.

Five seconds later, Diana finds her. "Maggie! What the hell? Are you okay?"

Maggie shakes her head. "I can't breathe. It's too hot. I need air."

"Okay," Diana says. She fans Maggie's face with the notebook-sized souvenir program she's bought. The air feels cool and nice, and for a second, Maggie thinks about telling Diana about her dad. Maybe she would understand. Maybe she'd say, "I had no idea either!" or, "Jeez, you really ARE stupid. Everyone knows. How come you couldn't see it?" Maybe she could tell Maggie how you let go, how you move on.

Diana's eyes narrow. "Oh my god, you're not gonna pass out, are you?" she says, sounding panicked, and the moment is gone.

Justine and Holly rush out of the concert hall, trailing a loud blast of music in their wake. "What's the matter?"

"Maggie needs air. We're going," Diana announces.

Holly glances toward the section doors. "But

they haven't even played 'I Want You to Want Me' yet. You know that'll be the encore."

"You can go back in. I'm okay," Maggie says, taking two shaky breaths. "I'm okay," she says again, trying to convince herself.

"We can ask them to play it for us later when we meet them," Diana says to Justine.

They've reached the doors, and security warns them that once they leave the arena, they can't come back in.

"We know the drill," Diana gripes. They step outside. It's pretty warm, but not as stifling as it was in the arena. Maggie takes a steadying breath and feels her body returning to normal. Behind them the concert hall vibrates with sound. It's the encore. "I Want You to Want Me."

"Your brother better be right about this, Maggie," Justine grumbles. "Or I am going to be super pissed."

★ ★ ★

By eleven thirty, the concert is over. Rowdy crowds of rockers swarm the parking lot of

Reunion Arena in T-shirts worn like coats of arms, showing their allegiances to the clans of Led Zeppelin, Bad Company, Styx, or Pink Floyd. Maggie has come in her own badge, a black-and-white Cheap Trick tee she bought on the last tour. A long-haired guy (clan of The Who) gives them a thumbs-up. "All right, man. Don't smoke it all."

The girls race to the ramp that leads into the loading area of the arena, hoping for a glimpse of the band or at least their bus. Several girls line the ramp. Dressed in black spandex and high heels, with crimped hair and dark eyeliner, they seem older, though one looks to be about Maggie's age. But there is something magical about them. They exude secret knowledge. They exude sex.

"Groupies," Diana spits.

"Those pants are so tight," Holly whispers, squinting. "You'd think she'd have panty lines."

"Duh, they're not wearing panties," Justine says.

A fat guy with a walkie-talkie and an all-access badge waves the groupies down the ramp but stops Maggie and her friends. "Y'all cain't be here.

This is a restricted area."

"Is Cheap Trick coming out here?" Maggie asks.

He shakes his head. "Concert's over, sweetheart. Y'all need to get on home now."

"Come on. Please?" Diana flashes her I-want-peppermint-schnapps smile.

The man folds his arms across his chest. He will not be moved. Behind him, one of the groupies flips them the bird before stepping through the privileged door to Wonderland.

"Assholes," Diana says.

The girls push through the crowds in the parking lot. It's a madhouse of revelers high on pot and music. Three guys in Live at Budokan tees sing "Surrender" at the top of their lungs. They dance in front of the girls, cutting them off until they can be cajoled into joining in with the chorus.

"*Mommy's all right, Daddy's all right, they just seem a little we-e-eird. Surrender, SURRENDER! But don't give yourselves awa-a-ay, awa-a-ay— aaaa-aa-e-ay!*"

The guys break into applause. The one with a

scraggly mustache says, "Hey, y'all wanna party? We've got—"

But whatever he says next is drowned out. The night is alive with honking horns, whoops and hollers, car radios blasting a late-night collage of guitar solos, wailing singers, drumbeats, and smoky DJ voices. It ignites something primal inside them, a need to howl at the moon, to brand the night and make it theirs. The girls join the chorus of shouts.

"Cheap Trick! Cheap Trick! Cheap Trick!" they call.

Laughing, Maggie loops her arm through Diana's, and they make their way toward the Hyatt.

★ ★ ★

The Hyatt Regency sits beside a lighted dome tower that cuts into the city's skyline like a weird architectural dandelion. There's a revolving restaurant at the top of the tower, but they could never afford to eat there. The only person they know who's ever been is Cecil Henderson, whose dad is a pilot for Braniff.

They've smoked half a joint in the car—not

much, just enough to give them all a pleasant buzz and a case of the giggles. They've sprayed themselves liberally with a bottle of Love's Baby Soft that Holly carries in her purse because she has a primordial fear of having B.O. But it's her special perfume, and she's upset that they've used so much of it.

"It's not that I mind or anything," she says, as they walk toward the Hyatt's glass doors. "It's just that I had to use my babysitting money for it."

"We didn't even use that much," Justine scoffs.

"At that Barbizon modeling class I took? They said you should spray the air and then walk into the perfume so you don't get too much. That's all I'm saying."

"They weren't getting high in the backseat of a car," Diana says, rolling her eyes.

Holly smiles. It's what they taught her at Barbizon, and she's never forgotten it. She smiles while her mother, the picture-of-the-Pope-on-the-dining-room-wall super-Catholic, tells her she'll be going to a Catholic girls' school next year. She smiles when she has to look after her five younger brothers and sisters on the weekends. She even smiled when she told them about her older sister, Mary, getting pregnant and being sent off to the Edna Gladney home for unwed mothers, though, truthfully, Holly could have been smiling about finally getting Mary's room, which is the attic, away from everyone else.

"I just hope it doesn't smell too strong," Holly mumbles.

The rumor that the band will be staying here has gotten around. A crowd of about thirty or forty fans mills around in the lobby, and the security team keeps coming over to throw them out. There's no hope of getting past the lobby—not even cute girls with quick smiles can charm the concierge and well-trained staff—so they take refuge behind a huge trough of potted ferns. The ferns are fake, but it's hard to tell at first glance. Someone has even oiled the leaves to give them a just-watered sheen.

"What do we do now?" Justine whispers.

"We wait," Maggie answers. "Pretend we're staying here."

Holly chews her bottom lip, casts a nervous glance toward the desk clerk handing a room key to a man in a three-piece suit. "What if they stop us? What if they ask what we're doing here?"

"We'll say we're here with our parents and we're supposed to meet them in the restaurant," Diana says.

A bellboy walks past pulling a luggage trolley, and Diana says to Justine loudly, "Your mom sure is taking a long time in the bathroom."

"She has female trouble," Justine says back, and the bellboy hurries on his way.

When the lobby fills with people, the girls see their chance. They break away and wander around the hotel, darting in and out of the gift shop, the restaurant, the piano lounge. In the lounge, a group of Japanese businessmen sits at a table beside a large tank filled with fish bright as gumballs. The businessmen stand and wave Maggie and her friends over. They offer to buy them drinks. Mai tais. Banana daquiris. Piña coladas. Drinks with names as exotic as a travel brochure. Vacations in glasses topped off with souvenir paper umbrellas, lacquered cherries.

The girls exchange quick glances.

"Will you excuse us? We'll be right back," Diana assures them before ushering the girls into the ladies' room for an impromptu huddle, a game plan. They busy themselves with fluffing and preening. Justine throws her head forward, shakes her head vigorously. When she stands up, her hair falls around her shoulders like thick folds of silk. "Oh my god, y'all," she says, putting one more coat of mascara on her spidery lashes. "Those guys must be seriously rich. Those mai tais are, like, four dollars each!"

"Free drinks!" Holly says, and she and Justine high-five.

Maggie hugs her purse to her middle. "What if they want us to go up to their room?"

"Do you think they would?" Holly asks, wide-eyed.

Diana shrugs. She pulls a tube of pink gloss from her purse and swipes the wand over her lips till they gleam with cheap drugstore sparkles. It's the one thing of her mother's she kept after Mrs. Tatum left to find herself at an ashram in Santa Fe. Her dad boxed up every last trace of her—the bottles of Avon rose eau de toilette, the Sears family photos, the macramé projects, half-finished canvases, David Bowie albums, sedatives still in their pill bottles, and broken sunglasses—and dropped it off at Goodwill, where the surprised church workers had no idea what to make of it all. "We've donated her life," Diana said, and she and her dad never spoke of it again.

Diana corrects a lip-gloss smudge with her pinkie nail. "We'll let them buy us some drinks, then we'll excuse ourselves for the bathroom and ditch 'em."

"What if they won't let us go?" Holly asks.

Diana gives her a hard look in the mirror. "Anybody can be ditched. You just walk away and you don't look back."

★★★

The businessmen stand when they return, and Justine beams as one of the men pushes her seat in for her. They seem a lot older to Maggie now that she can get a good look at them, about her dad's age. The one sitting closest to has uneven teeth stained with nicotine.

"I don't think we should do this," Maggie whispers to Diana, who's studying the drink menu.

"Would you relax?" Diana snaps.

Under the table, Maggie slips a hand into her Levi's pocket and traces the outline of the dime there.

Justine cups a hand to Maggie's ear. "Order a mai tai. They're good."

Justine's comfortable in places like this. Her parents are professors, and they don't care what she does as long as her grades are good. Once her mom caught her smoking cigarettes in the backyard, and all she did was hand her an empty Coke can for the butts. Mostly, her parents travel, leaving casseroles in the freezer and the numbers of the hotels where they'll be staying. Sometimes they forget to leave the numbers.

The waitress makes her slow march to the table.

She has tightly permed hair with straight bangs in a wall across her forehead. She looks like she could be someone's grandma; her skin crinkles at her elbows, and Maggie swallows hard, pretends to be bored instead of scared.

"Four mai tais, two wine, one whiskey sour," the man with the bad teeth says.

The waitress shifts her weight and cocks a hip, and Maggie feels it in the quickening of her pulse. "I'll need to see some ID from you ladies."

"Sure," Diana says. She rifles through her purse. "Oh my gosh, y'all. I can't find my wallet! I hope I left it in the car!"

"I cain't serve y'all without proper identification." The waitress draws out all six syllables.

"I'm twenty-one," Diana says.

Maggie grabs Diana's hand under the table. "Let's just go," she whispers.

The businessman intercedes. "Twenty-one. Okay? Okay." He points from girl to girl. "Twenty-one. Twenty-one."

The waitress's lips press into a tight line.

"Twenty-one, my eye. I may have been born on a Wednesday, but it wasn't last Wednesday. You girls need to get out of here."

The girls don't argue and they don't wait. There is a mad grab for purses while the Japanese businessman keeps saying twenty-one; they manage an indignant saunter from the lounge, and then they break into a run, not stopping until they are in the lobby doubled over laughing.

"Oh my god, oh my GOD!" Justine says between great hiccuping laughs. "I thought we were toast!"

"We order drink for ladies," Diana says, being ridiculous. "Make them drunk for fucky-sucky."

Holly screeches and clamps a hand over her mouth, removing it just as quickly. "Oh gross, gross, GROSS!"

"They didn't sound like that, Diana," Maggie says, rolling her eyes.

"Fucky-sucky," Justine echoes, snickering.

It's like dominoes then. Holly laughs, and finally Maggie has to laugh too. They move down the fluorescent corridor, arms linked, the Four

Musketeers of Suburbia, smiling brightly to passers-by, who look confused and slightly suspicious.

★ ★ ★

They take the elevator to the sixth floor and walk the hall. A room service tray sits abandoned on the floor beside a closed door. The silver cover has been cast aside, revealing a forlorn half-eaten omelet, miniature salt and pepper shakers, two empty Dr Pepper cans, a lipstick-stained coffee cup, and an untouched piece of toast. Justine plucks the toast from the plate and takes a bite.

"What?" she says through a mouthful of bread. "I've got the munchies."

A maid has left the door open to room 617. They stand on the threshold and peer in at the neat double beds, the matching bedside tables, the lamps turned to low. Justine is the first in, always up for a dare.

"Close the door," Diana whispers, and Holly locks it.

Maggie is afraid to touch anything. Her mother

would be beyond disappointed if she knew what Maggie was up to. She knows her mother is asleep right now, nestled under her flowered comforter. Snug. Safe. A part of Maggie wishes she were there, too.

Justine falls back onto the bed with her arms outstretched. "This is sooo comfortable. What do you suppose it costs to stay here?"

"A gajillion dollars," Diana says. She flips the light on in the bathroom. "There's good stuff in here."

They congregate in the bathroom, where Diana rips the sanitized paper doily from the water glass and fills it with water from the tap. "Ew, Dallas water is so hard. Too mineraly. Look, little soaps."

She pockets one, and then they take the complimentary bottles of shampoo and conditioner, the body lotion, and two more tiny boxed soaps, dropping them into Holly's purse.

Justine pulls the plastic shower cap from its paper sheath and tucks all her hair up into it till she looks like a giant mushroom.

"Now, don't be home late," she says, adopting a motherly tone.

"Oh my god," Diana laughs. "That should be your senior picture."

"It IS gonna be my senior picture—just you wait," Justine says. "In fact, I'm gonna wear this in pictures from now on. You will never see me without it."

Diana falls back on the bed laughing, and that's all the encouragement Justine needs. She squinches up her eyes and makes her voice funny again. "Have you girls been smoking marijuana? Hmmm? Don't you know it's the devil's weed?"

"I'm sorry, Mom," Maggie says. "I'll never do it again. It's strictly cocaine from now on."

"That's better," Justine says.

Holly leafs through the hotel's tourist guide, with its vivid ads for steak houses and high-end dress shops. "Does your mom wear one of those, Jussie?"

Justine shrugs. "How would I know?" She takes the cap off and combs through her hair with her fingers, patting it smooth. "Where the hell is the band, anyway?"

"David said they'd be here," Maggie assures them, but she's begun to wonder herself.

"Can't you call him up, ask him?"

"I don't know where he is," Maggie says, and for the first time she realizes she hasn't talked to her brother since Tuesday.

Diana opens the minibar. Inside is a dazzling array of doll-sized liquor bottles. "Oooh, Tanqueray," she says. She takes four bottles and hands them out like party favors. Maggie gets a bottle of bourbon, which is her dad's drink. She unscrews the top and takes a quick sip. It goes down hot and bitter but fades to a full-body warmth. The four of them lie on one bed, drinking and staring at the ceiling, talking about the concert, which songs were best.

"Mags, doesn't your dad live somewhere around here?" Justine asks suddenly.

"In Oak Lawn," Maggie answers.

"Oak Lawn." Holly yawns. "Isn't that where all the queers live?"

Maggie's heart beats a little faster. "Not everybody who lives there is."

Justine chucks her empty rum bottle toward the trash can, and it lands on the carpet. "Shit."

She sits up and Diana pulls her back down. "Just leave it for the maid."

"What do you suppose two guys do together?" Justine asks.

"What do you think?" Diana makes a hole with her thumb and index finger and slides her other index finger in and out of it quickly.

Holly and Justine shriek. "Ewww, grody!"

"You are so disgusting, Diana," Justine says, but she's laughing.

Maggie curls up on the bed with her knees to her chest and imagines herself sinking down to the bottom of the pool. She closes her eyes and sees the shadowy sanctuary taking shape—the shiny diamonds of light in the water, the prickly white concrete floor, the thick black numbers around the sides showing the depth, letting you know where you stood.

"Maggie!" Holly snaps.

Maggie opens her eyes. "What?"

"I said does your dad have a new girlfriend yet?"

"No. Not yet." Maggie sits up. She starts to tuck the bourbon into her jeans, thinks better of it, and leaves it in the nightstand drawer. "I have to whiz, and then we should probably get out of here before we get caught."

"I don't think the band's gonna show," Justine says, yawning again.

Diana checks the bedside clock radio. "Fifteen more minutes."

"If I stay here, I'm gonna fall asleep," Justine mumbles.

★ ★ ★

The girls ride the glass elevators to the top of Reunion Tower. The city falls away beneath them. From up where they are, everything looks squashed, flung from the hand of a disappointed god. Maggie has seen pictures of other cities—New York and Singapore, London, Paris. She likes the way the buildings look all pushed against each other, each one holding the others up whether they like it or not. Dallas isn't like that. It's more a big marbles game, houses and malls and glass office buildings thrown out in a random pattern, nothing touching. There's so much space, you feel like you could drown in it.

Maggie presses her face against the glass and peers out at the night—the blurry neon lights, the cars streaming over the network of freeways, the neat yellow test pattern of house windows lit against the dark. She wonders if she could pick out her dad's condo in Oak Lawn, the one he shares with a man named Bill, who is his lover and has been for six months now.

★ ★ ★

After the divorce, Maggie and her mother moved into a California-style townhouse in a fading section of town where the streets were used as makeshift garages. There were always cars in various stages of repair parked in front of the houses, and when the cars were gone, or the men took off for good, they left behind patchy oil stains, black wounds in the asphalt that never completely healed.

"It has a nice window seat," her mother said cheerily when she showed Maggie her room—a long, narrow rectangle with a unicorn-and-rainbow mural painted on one wall.

"That's gotta go," Maggie said, settling her milk crate full of albums, the only thing she didn't trust to the movers, on the green shag carpeting.

"The girl who lived here before was an artist," her mother said. "She got a scholarship to a very prestigious art school in Oklahoma, I think. You could have an original by a famous artist on your wall!"

It was so like her mother to try to erase it all with a comment, like putting a big yellow happy-face sticker on shit.

"It is physically impossible to have an art school in Oklahoma. It would cause a ripple in time or something," Maggie said.

Her mother sighed. "Well, you don't have to be ugly about it." *I'm not mad, just disappointed.*

Maggie took a good look at the room. Faint pencil marks were etched beside the doorjamb, small lines with height measurements and dates out to the side. Maggie followed the growth chart from three feet, ten inches up to five feet, four inches, which was Maggie's height. There were whole years in those marks—a history that couldn't be boxed up and taken along. Some parts of yourself you just had to leave behind.

Maggie scratched at the marks with her thumbnail, making them into an indecipherable smudge. "What happened to the people who lived here before?"

"The mother got remarried to a man in the Air Force, and he got transferred to Kansas. Or maybe it was Nevada. Kansas or Nevada. I'll have to ask Maureen about it." Her mother pulled a KISS album from the crate, scowled, and put it back. "I think the mother was a registered dietician with the school system, so she can get a job anywhere. That's a really smart thing to have in your back pocket. Something to fall back on, so if your husband gets transferred somewhere else, you can always get a job."

"I'm never getting married," Maggie said.

Her mother crossed her arms. "You know what happened is nobody's fault, Maggie. There are no villains here."

"Wow, that's great, Mom. Did you read that on a poster?" It was a terrible thing to say, but Maggie needed a villain. A villain would help.

"I'm going to unpack the kitchen," her mother said. She gave the milk crate a shove with her foot on the way out.

Alone in her room, Maggie pulled a Magic Marker from her pocket and drew a mustache on the unicorn so that he was in disguise, just like everyone else.

Her brother had called in the evening to see how the move went.

"There's a goddam unicorn on my bedroom wall," Maggie said.

"Horny Gas & Oil. Put a little unicorn in your tank and see what you've been myth-ing!" her brother shouted. Maggie could hear a party in the background. Drums. Girls laughing. A guitar string bent into a sweet pain of sound.

"Where are you?" Maggie asked.

"Some chick's house in Houston. It was a great gig, man—you shoulda been here."

"Time Travel Airlines. For when you absolutely, positively have to be there yesterday."

"What?" her brother shouted.

"TIME TRAVEL AIR—"

"Hold on," her brother said. She could hear him yelling at someone in the room. "Hey man, save some for me."

"David?" she said. She wanted to ask him when he was coming home. If he would take her with him. She wanted to ask him how he knew about their dad, if there were ways you could always know when it's ending—signs to look for, insider information—so that you wouldn't be caught off guard with a crate full of albums in a room that would never feel like yours.

Some girl was laughing and telling David to

come on, and Maggie had that feeling again, like she'd stayed too long on the bottom of the pool.

"Hey, Mags, I gotta go," he said. "Stay cool, man."

"Stay Cool Deodorant. Give your B.O. the cold shoulder," Maggie said breathlessly, but the line had already gone dead.

★ ★ ★

The girls canvas the lobby one last time, but there's no sign of the band, and the fans who have been waiting around have mostly cleared out by now. Only a few remain at the doors, white scraps of paper in their hands, cameras at the ready. But they're already talking about next month's concert, and Maggie can tell their hearts aren't in it anymore. They just don't want to admit defeat.

They stumble out to the car, tired, a little drunk, deflated. The adrenaline-fueled light-headedness Maggie felt early in the evening has been replaced by a heavy weight, as if she were trying to move underwater. She has a dull headache from the pot and the booze, and her eyes are scratchy. The parking lot of Reunion Arena is dotted with empty beer cans, trampled ticket stubs, bits of paper. It's a ghost world, and it seems amazing to Maggie that only a few hours ago it was mayhem.

"I could kill your stupid brother," Justine grouses. She's carrying her shoes in her hand.

"They might still show," Maggie says, even though she doesn't believe it. It's something her mom would say.

Now that their high has worn off, they are hungry. Starving. Impossibly ravenous. They would eat whole plates of pancakes and French fries, burgers and omelets. They ride in search of someplace to eat, no mean feat at four in the morning. Just off Cedar Springs Road they find an all-night diner, the Sunrise. It's a low, flat building with fake stone and boxy windows that look out onto traffic. They park in the back and take a booth in the corner near the restrooms.

The only other customers are four Mexican busboys just off shift, still in their IHOP aprons, a couple of working girls, and a grizzled man in a rumpled windbreaker who pours sugar into a spoon and dumps it into his iced tea again and again, mumbling to himself the whole time. Maggie figures him to be one of those crazy Vietnam vets who hang out in downtown Dallas at the intersections washing car windows for money. This guy isn't trying to wash windows. He's just smoking cigarettes and talking softly to himself while he arranges his silverware in a specific pattern.

The waitress brings them tall, slick menus and ice water in brown plastic glasses. Maggie wants to resist eating. She's been dieting, trying to get rid of the hips and boobs, the womanly softness that's creeping up on her while she sleeps like some silent dust storm, so that every morning when she wakes, nothing is what it used to be, and she has to relearn the landscape of her body.

Her mother clucks sympathetically when Maggie mentions this to her. "Oh honey, you got the Struber thighs, I'm afraid." And for just a minute, Maggie feels this thin thread connecting them. They starve themselves in solidarity, smiling ruefully over meals of iceberg lettuce and Alba 66 shakes, Tab soda, cottage cheese, plain, tasteless hamburger patties without the bun or even a dab of mayonnaise, salmon from a can.

"You should eat the bones—they're good for you. Calcium," her mother says, pointing to the tiny round bobbin of bone in the pinky, mushy middle. Maggie crunches the bone into pulp between her back teeth, and she and her mother talk about school and work and clothes and maybe buying a piano if her mom does well at her Amway job.

"They give you bonuses," her mother says, spooning green Jell-O onto the dessert plates that came with her wedding china. "Might as well use them. Seems a shame to pack them away," she says, carrying the wobbly gelatin carefully to the table, watching for signs that it might make a run for it.

Maggie eats these meals for as long as she can, until she feels her hunger is an enraged animal living inside her. Then she rides her bike to the 7-Eleven and gorges on Twinkies, Ding-Dongs, Dr Pepper, and bags of Doritos that leave her fingers stained an unnatural orange. She rides away from these secret feasts full but never satisfied.

"What'll you have, hon?" the waitress asks.

"I'll have the cheeseburger. With fries. And, um, a side of mayo, please," Maggie says quickly. Tomorrow she will be good. She will eat water-packed tuna on Melba toast and go for a run. Tomorrow she will be her mother's daughter.

The waitress brings their drinks and a plate of fries to start.

"That was such a rip-off," Justine says, propping her chin up with her palm. "They never even showed up. I'll bet they're not staying there at all. I'll bet they're at the Adolphus."

Maggie shrugs. "Maybe they changed their minds."

"Maybe David is full of shit." Justine blows the little white paper cover from her straw and it lands in Maggie's water, so she has to fish it out.

"Man, I'm wasted," Diana giggles. "Are y'all wasted?"

Holly laughs. "Totally."

Diana salts the fries without asking. "Mag-a-Doodle, we're in Oak Lawn. Is your dad's place near here?"

"Kind of. I think it's not that close, actually." Maggie scoops up a piece of ice and drops it in her mouth, filling it completely.

"We could stay there."

"I thaw we wuh stayn a' yo howth," Maggie manages through the ice.

"I can' drive back. I'm too wasted," Diana says. Her eyes are red, her skin flushed.

"I'll drive," Justine offers.

"You can't drive stick," Diana says, and Justine sulks over her Pepsi.

"Hey, check out that guy in the corner," Maggie says, hoping to change the subject. "Attractive."

Diana stares at her. "Why can' we stay there? I mean, he's still yer dad, isn' he?"

Maggie fishes for ice, but the slivers are too thin; they slip out of her fingers. "I can't show up at, like, four in the morning with all my friends, sorta drunk. Besides, it's not even his place. He's renting from this guy." Her cheeks warm, and she hopes they can't read the lie in her face: *No, Officer, I had no idea the speed limit was twenty-five. Of course I'm eighteen. I didn't skip physics— I got my period and had to leave school, Mom.* "We'll be fine once we eat."

Diana purses her lips. "I don' see why you can't jus' call him."

Holly and Justine look to her hopefully.

"It's just . . . I just can't, okay? Can you pass the ketchup?" Maggie doesn't wait but reaches for it, and Diana holds it away.

"Call him."

"Can I please have the ketchup?"

Diana waves the ketchup wildly, nearly hitting one of the IHOP busboys in the head. She's making the fall from fun drunk into belligerent drunk.

"Give me the ketchup or I'll tell that guy you're in love with him." Maggie points to the rumpled man in the corner, who is stuffing Sweet 'n Low packets into his pockets.

Diana takes the bait. "You mean your boyfriend?"

"Your boyfriend. Your one true love," Maggie says, relieved. She has Diana now. "I'm so jealous of your hunk of man meat."

"Oh, gross!" Diana says, laughing so hard, a fleck of mushy French fry flies from her lips and lands on Holly's Pepsi glass. Holly yelps, flinging it away like a booger, and this only makes them laugh all the harder.

"M-m-man m-m-meat," Justine laughs, her voice spiraling into the stratosphere.

The waitress brings their food and they tear into it eagerly, pausing only for further insults and gross-outs. And Maggie plays hardest, keeping herself safe behind a wall of laughter.

★★★

By the time they finish their meals, it's clear that Diana is totally wasted. Instead of sobering her up, the food seems to have made her even drunker. In the diner's back parking lot she's holding on to a stack of tires, her underwear stretched between her wobbly ankles.

"Just go inside and use the restroom," Holly says.

"Can' make it," Diana slurs. "Block me." The girls form a human wall in front of Diana, who pees, loses her balance, and falls down into the puddle with a yelp and a laugh.

"Oh, GER-OSS!" Justine screeches. Diana grabs her wrist and tries to pull her down into it, too, and Holly shushes them both.

"Y'all, stop it! Someone's gonna see!"

Diana's lips curl into a sneer. "Yer such a priss, Holly. Such a good li'l Catholic girl."

"I am not." Holly can't stop smiling. It's like she's stuck.

"Such a Goody Two-shoes. Bet yer mom would never leave such a good, good girl."

"My mom hates me. I'm just free babysitting," Holly says. She laughs, but her eyes are watery.

Justine rustles in her purse for tissues, which she gives to Diana, who wipes and pulls up her wet undies.

"I can' wear these," she says, and throws them to the ground. "Happy birthday, perverts."

The single bulb over the Sunrise's back door

bleeds out, casting yellow light over their tired faces. Justine's mascara has left black rings under her eyes like a raccoon.

"How are we gonna get home?" she asks.

"Fucky-sucky," Diana giggles. "Fucky-sucky, fucky-sucky."

"Shhh, don't," Holly says, and suddenly she's crying, and Maggie thinks of the dime in her inner jeans pocket.

★ ★ ★

The Sunrise has a pay phone up near the front counter with its cash register, toothpick dispenser, and bowl full of creamy mints. Maggie slides inside the narrow phone booth and closes the door. Scribbles in different pen colors, different scripts, litter the wall:

For a good time, call Jenny.

Just because you're paranoid doesn't mean they're not out to get you.

"It's okay to look outside
The day it will abide
And watch the sunrise."
            —Big Star

If you're here, where am I?
If you're not here, where are you?

She dials his number. It rings once, twice, four times. On the fifth ring, a man's voice answers with a sleepy "Hullo?" She twists the cord around her index finger till the tip turns a fat purple.

"Who is this?" the man asks, more demanding this time.

"Is my dad there?" Maggie answers.

"Oh," the man says. And then again, "Oh. Hold on."

The phone is fumbled; static fills her ears. She hears muffled voices and then her dad is on the line.

"Maggie? Baby? What's wrong?"

"Sorry, Daddy. Did I wake you up?"

"No, it's . . . okay." Her dad's voice is deep and raw

with sleep. "Is something wrong? Is your mom okay?"

"No. I mean, yeah, she's fine. I'm in Dallas. I went to a concert." Everything she says sounds like a question. She takes a deep breath. "I'm in Oak Lawn."

"You're here?"

"Yeah. We're at a diner. The Sunrise."

She hears her dad say to Bill, "They're at the Sunrise. I know, I know," and then he's back on the line. "The Sunrise, huh? Charming establishment. Kind of like a bad prison movie. Is Olivia de Havilland there?"

"She's serving eggs and screaming about Joan Fontaine being a bitch."

"Ah." Her dad chuckles.

Maggie wraps her finger completely in its phone-cord cocoon. "Um, Diana's too drunk to take the wheel, and nobody else can drive stick."

"Do you need me to come get you?"

"No, that's okay," she says, a reflex. She stares at a spot on the wall where someone has scrawled a response to an earlier question in red ink:

*You are here. We all are. We just
can't see it.*

The words squiggle and blur, and she blinks
hard against the tears that show up uninvited. The
whole cruddy night implodes inside her chest,
bringing her defenses down on themselves in a
whoosh of choking dust. She is all that is left standing, a small piece of rubble that has escaped the
blast. "I was just wondering . . . maybe it would be
better if we could crash at your apartment?"

It's quiet for a second or two, long enough for
Maggie to want to take it back.

"Hold on." Her dad puts the phone to his
chest. She can hear it sliding against his pajama
top, making a crackling sound. She wants him to
say, yes, yes, of course you can come, you don't
even have to ask. But it isn't like that anymore. It
isn't even her dad's place. None of them really
have a place. They're tethered by this impossible
silence, interrupted only by static and jokes and
muffled talk, held motionless by the things that

can't be said to one another.

Outside, the sky's pinkening. A newspaper truck idles in front of the Sunrise. A guy shoves a neatly folded stack of morning papers into the glass-front case beside the door and drives away. She hears her dad's voice again. "Give us fifteen minutes."

The drive to Bill's condo is only a mile. Maggie takes the wheel, and Holly works the stick. When the engine starts to sound like it's gargling nails, Maggie shouts, "Shift!" and Holly works the gearshift into second or third and back down again at traffic lights, which are on some insane timer that they cannot seem to beat. In the backseat, Diana yells, "Shift! Shift!" over and over again, laughing maniacally.

"Stop it, Diana," Holly says. "You're confusing me!"

But Diana only says it more.

Maggie's nerves are shot. She wants the night to be over. She wants Diana to be quiet so she can drive. She wants her dad.

"Diana," Maggie snaps, "we're going to strip all

the gears if you don't shut up."

Diana's head lolls against the backseat. Her lips tremble. "Please don't fuck up my car. It never did anything to you," she says, and bursts into tears.

After two wrong turns, Maggie finally finds her dad's street. It's a long one flanked mostly by apartment buildings with names like The Windsor and Royal Court. Her dad lives in a coral stucco complex called The Chapparel. Maggie parks out front, and she and Holly prop Diana onto their shoulders and half drag her through an interior courtyard with a rock garden and some kind of exotic cactus. Justine trails behind, carrying their purses.

"I'm gonna puke," Diana moans.

"Not yet you're not," Maggie warns.

"Oh god, oh god," Diana's eyes flutter.

"Not yet," Maggie says. "Almost there."

Maggie finds the door, number 7B, and knocks softly. The door opens.

"Hi, Daddy," Maggie says.

"Oh god," Diana says, and vomits all over the carpet.

★ ★ ★

A half hour later Diana is passed out on the bathroom floor, her arm wrapped around the toilet base like a cherished friend. Justine and Holly have been put into the second bedroom under blankets Maggie recognizes, blankets that used to be in their linen closet at home. It's just Maggie and her dad and Bill on the long camel-back sofa across from a wall of mirrors. She sees them reflected there like those speak-no-evil monkeys on a cigarette break. Bill has thrown on a terry-cloth robe that's gone flat with washing. Her dad is dressed in jeans and a T-shirt. His auburn hair sticks up in stiff tufts that might look rocker cool except that it's her dad and so it doesn't. His eyes are the same heavy-lidded blue as hers but older, like a time-lapse photography exhibit of her next twenty-five years.

Bill isn't what she expected. He's solidly built, like he could have played football when he was younger but now he's got a little bit of a belly on him. His face is soft and shadowy with stubble. He wears cheap brown plastic glasses. Put a white button-down on him and he'd look like any bean counter in an accounting firm.

"The place is nice," Maggie says, eyeing the dinette set in the corner, the arched chrome lamp, the china cabinet housing shiny white plates and bottles of wine, all of it Bill's, all of it foreign.

"Would you like a soda or some tea?" Bill asks. "I've got some oolong."

Maggie doesn't know what oolong is, but she wants to be agreeable so she says yes. She follows her dad and his lover into the bright white kitchen. Bill hands the kettle to her dad, who fills it under the faucet while Bill reaches into a cabinet for a box of tea bags. They move around each other in easy harmony, and the one time they screw up—Bill opens the fridge, and her dad nearly bumps into the open door—they grin as if it's some private joke they share. Maggie has seen her dad happy and sad, pissed off and preoccupied, but she's never seen him this way. She does not yet know this dad, the one moving so easily around his kitchen, handing his lover eggs to crack in a bowl, taking a milk carton from his hand and placing it back in the fridge. He has unpacked someone new here, and she will have to learn the way of him.

Her dad licks a dollop of sour cream from his fingers, and Bill automatically extends a dish towel.

Maggie clears her throat. "Um, I thought I'd go see the pool."

"Swim hours aren't until eight," her dad explains.

"I was just gonna stick my feet in. If that's okay."

Her dad looks to Bill, who shrugs.

"As long as you're quiet, nobody really cares," Bill says.

The pool is only a few feet from her dad's condo. It's a long, chemically blue rectangle surrounded by a white metal fence and lots of lounge chairs. Maggie sits at the edge of the deep end and tests it with her toes. It's still holding some of yesterday's heat, warm as a bath. It would be a good place to spend a summer afternoon, maybe as good as the Holiday Inn.

A flight attendant emerges from one of the

second-floor apartments. She stands on the balcony in her crisp navy uniform and matching pumps, a rolling weekender bag at her feet. She smiles at a businessman four doors down stepping out with his briefcase, a newspaper under his arm. They do not call each other by name but wave and smile and say good morning before heading in different directions, to different commutes. One by one, people come out of their dark, mysterious caves, blinking against the new light—a runner off for his morning jog, a scruffy guy in his boxers scratching his belly, a woman in sensible work shoes, two kids in tow. They go and come back and go again. No one stays for long.

Her dad has come out. He sits next to her, a glass of orange juice in his hand, and places the steaming tea mug beside her.

"Nice pool," Maggie says. "Very Sunset Boulevard."

Her dad does an exaggerated Gloria Swanson face, all curled lips and big, crazy eyes. "It's the pictures that got small!"

"Anybody up yet?" Maggie asks.

"Sleeping. In another few hours they'll be praying for death."

Maggie imagines her friends waking up in a few hours, looking around at the condo, putting it all together. They'll know, and maybe Maggie should care about that, but she doesn't.

"I guess I should call Mom," she says.

Her dad sips his juice. "Already done. I let her know you were here."

In her mind, Maggie can see her mother sitting alone at the kitchen table in her pale-green nylon robe, her paper spread out, a cup of Sanka sitting beside her in a mug decorated with Christmas cats, the words SANTA CLAWS LIVES HERE emblazoned around the rim, the numbing hum of the central air providing a soundtrack. If Maggie were home, she'd be slurping her Cheerios while her mom chattered nervously about things that didn't matter. Her mother doesn't trust silence. Maggie wonders if her mother is talking even now though no one is there to hear it, if she's still afraid of what could settle around her in that empty space if she doesn't keep filling it. It's a terrible responsibility, trying to keep them all safe from the unsaid, and Maggie feels bad about it. She should talk more, take some of the burden away. She vows to be nicer to her mom when she gets home, and even as she makes the promise to herself, she knows she will break it.

Maggie cups her eyes with her hands to block the morning sun. "Is she pissed?"

Her father shrugs, sips his coffee. "Surprised. Glad you're okay."

Surprised. Disappointed. Concerned.

"Did you tell her everything?"

He nods solemnly. "Yes, and she's going to take your left ear, which she'll keep in a jar by her bed. Let that be a lesson to you."

Maggie winces. "Did you really tell her?"

Her dad shakes his head. "I told her you were too tired to drive back so you came here instead. The truth, the partial truth, and nothing but the truth."

"Thanks," Maggie says.

"*De nada.*"

Across the pool, Bill stands at the condo's kitchen window rinsing glasses, watching them. She's made a hell of a first impression.

Maggie holds the mug in her hands. It's hot against her palms, but she likes it. "I thought maybe I could spend some weekends once school's out. You could tell people I'm a Bolivian circus contortionist you won in a poker game with missionaries."

"Those missionaries. They can't hold their liquor, and they always lose at cards."

"Ain't it the truth," Maggie says, but she's starting to tear up. She takes a steadying breath and asks again. "Would it be okay?"

Upstairs, the mother is back without her kids. Looking frazzled and annoyed, she rushes into her apartment and comes out seconds later holding a tattered rabbit by the ear. Maggie listens to the woman's heels click down the stairs and away while she waits for her dad to answer for real. The waiting is hard, and she has to bite her lip to keep from making a joke or talking about old movies, anything to break the silence.

"I think we could arrange it," he says at last.

She sips the oolong. It has a taste like grass, sharp and clean. It's not bad, just different. She thinks she could get used to it.

Her dad rises, stretches his arms against the hazy light of morning. "You coming in?"

Maggie shakes her head. "Not yet. It's nice out here."

"Okay. Bill's making waffles. They should be ready in about five minutes."

"Five-minute waffles . . ." Maggie starts to make a commercial, but nothing clever comes, and so she says what she feels. "Waffles sound good."

Her dad goes inside, and Maggie stays behind, sipping her tea, getting accustomed to it. The early-morning pink haze has given way to a blue growing steadily sharper. It's going to be hot. Maggie doesn't know what time it is—probably not near eight yet, though—but the pool is a happy blue, and Maggie can't wait. She slips into the warm water, letting her body adjust by degrees. She swims the sidestroke from one end to the other and back again, enjoying her easy buoyancy, the way the water moves against her cupped hands. When she stops for breath, her skin itches with chlorine, so she folds her arms and drops to the bottom like a stone. She hugs her knees to her chest and watches the air bubbles squeak out of her tightly closed lips. They float up toward the distorted world above. Maggie sits for as long as she can, feeling her lungs tighten, until she can't sit a moment longer. With one strong push, she arcs up, legs pumping, arms reaching out, grabbing hard for the surface.

She breaks through with an audible gasp, drawing as much air into her lungs as she can, inhaling more deeply than she can ever remember. It's like she's breathing all the way up from her toes, like every cell in her body is waking up and demanding air, and she can't do it here in the deep end with so much pressing against her. She needs to get out, anyway. The waffles should be ready.

Maggie swims toward the ladder. The sun's gaining strength; she can feel its coiled heat on her back. The day will be clear and hot. A good pool day. Maybe her friends will want to stay for a swim. They could lie on towels listening to the radio and drive home in the afternoon, when the traffic's not so bad and it's easier to talk.

A guy in shorts and a T-shirt lets himself in through the gate. He's carrying a pool sweeper in one hand. In the other is a caddy filled with bottles, chemicals to make the water sparkle like a desert hope.

"Sorry, miss, but I've got to clean it now," he says, smiling in apology.

Maggie smiles back. "That's okay. I was just going in."

She grabs hold of the metal rungs with sure hands and pulls herself up out of the warm, wavy blue, and the water falls off her like a million shards of glass.

INGALISA SCHROBSDORFF

Libba Bray is the *New York Times* bestselling author of A *Great and Terrible Beauty*, *Rebel Angels*, and *The Sweet Far Thing*. Her books were named ALA Best Books for Young Adults in 2005 and 2006. Before writing novels, Libba worked as a waitress, nanny, burrito roller, publishing plebe, and advertising copywriter, which may or may not explain her characters' love of television commercials. Libba was born in Alabama, grew up in Texas, and now lives in Brooklyn with her husband and their son. You can visit her online at www.libbabray.com.

THE
VULNERABLE
HOURS

David Levithan

Later, there would be people who would try to explain it away. There was something in the light, they'd say. The sky was a color that nobody had ever seen before, a rose-tinted darkness that made the air seem more tender to breathe. Other people would swear that the tincture in the air wasn't light or color but scent, an uncertain distillation of the things you were afraid to admit you desired. The temperature could not be blamed, because it was so mild that nobody felt it. Not a single person in the city shivered the entire night, nor did anyone feel overburdened by heat. Minds wandered to other things.

Sarah Wilkins may have been the first to feel it.

She was in her room, alone, getting ready to go out. She could hear her mother yelling at her sister in the kitchen—something about a lack of respect, probably stemming from the fact that Sarah's sister had taken to leaving without saying good-bye. Sarah drowned out the fight and focused on her face in the mirror. She tried not to feel sad about the acne on her forehead or the fact that her bangs were too long. *I just have to try to make it better*, she said to herself. And then she surprised herself by adding, *Why?* She put on her cover-up, her blush, her lipstick. She teased and gelled and pulled her bangs into shape. *It's a party*, she told herself. But the *why* still lingered.

Amanda called to say she and Ashley were two minutes away. Sarah was only going to the party because Amanda and Ashley wanted to. The guy who was throwing it was a complete jerk, and the guy Amanda wanted to see there wasn't much better. Sarah never told her this, because what was the use? When had a friend's opinion ever undone a crush?

Even worse, Amanda's crush had a friend. Sarah had already forgotten his name—or maybe nobody had bothered to mention it to her. All that mattered was that he was going to be at Devin's party. Amanda had even told her what to wear. Ever dutiful, Sarah had put on the skirt they'd bought at Bloomingdale's over spring break. Amanda had said Sarah looked good in it, but Sarah suspected she was only saying that so she'd feel less guilty about her own purchases.

"Aren't you excited?" Amanda and Ashley asked when Sarah met them in front of her building. Sarah didn't say it, but she realized she was the opposite of excited. Then she realized she didn't even know what the opposite of excited was. She'd never allowed herself to express it, so the word had just dissolved.

On the subway downtown, Amanda and Ashley gossiped about who was going to be at the party and then tried to guess what was going to happen. Sarah kept silent, not even realizing she was staring at the woman on the seat across from hers. The woman was alone, quietly reading a magazine. She looked like that was all she wanted for the moment, and she was content in having it. Sarah was surprised by how jealous she felt. She didn't know this woman; this woman was old. Why would Sarah simply assume a stranger's life was better than hers?

The boy throwing the party went to one of the private schools that didn't even bother to be named after a saint. He didn't greet them at the door. Instead, the girls found the door cracked open, a bare-bones invitation to walk from the hallway of the building into the hallway of the apartment. It was already crowded with teenagers—mostly anonymous, mostly drinking. Amanda and Ashley led the way, angling through the crowds until they found the bed with the coats on it. Then they angled again until they got to the place where the beer was being distributed. Sarah took a bottle, because it was handed to her. She said thank you, because it was the right thing to say. But she didn't take a sip, or even look around much. She noticed the copper pots hanging on the walls and wondered if they were ever used, or if they were just there for decoration. She asked Amanda, and Amanda either didn't hear or pretended not to. Instead, she and Ashley took sips from their bottles and scoped out the crowd. Sarah knew Amanda and Ashley were not going to leave her; they were in this together. This had always been a comfort to her, because she feared being left behind. But now, on this strange night, she wanted just that. She wanted them to forget she was there.

Sarah was not used to making excuses, so she fell back on the most universal one: She said she had to go to the restroom. That's how she said it— *restroom*—as if they were in a restaurant instead of some rich kid's home. Amanda and Ashley said they'd wait for her in the den; the jerk Amanda liked had last been seen heading that way, and Amanda didn't want to miss her chance.

Sarah didn't know which direction the bathroom was in, so she chose the direction opposite the one Amanda and Ashley were taking. It was still early in the evening, but already couples were making out against walls and boys were putting on their jackets to go to the roof for a smoke. Sarah wanted to put her unsipped beer bottle down, but all the available surfaces were too close to people. She had no desire to be pulled into a conversation. She just wanted to find a room where she could close the door and lock it and be alone.

Lindsay Weiss saw Sarah walking down the hall, looking into doorways, trying to find something. Lindsay would never have been able to explain it, but immediately she recognized what Sarah was feeling. She knew it as if it was happening to her. So she cut off the boy from Regency who was attempting to flirt with her, and she caught up with Sarah just as she was about to peer into a bedroom.

"Excuse me," she said to Sarah. "But you look lost."

Before, Sarah had felt stirrings, but they were isolated stirrings. Now, having this girl come up to her and say she looked lost, the stirrings filled her with noise. Not the noise of sound, but a noise much louder than that—the noise of thought.

"Yes, I'm lost," she said. And she could have left it at that. She could have just asked where the restroom was. But something about tonight made her go further, made her more honest than necessary. There was something in this girl's eyes that already understood. So Sarah found herself adding, "I'm completely lost. I don't belong here at all."

The truth feels different from other things. The closest you can come to describing it is that it feels like taking a perfect breath.

Without having to think about it, Lindsay knew the next thing to say was, "I'm Lindsay."

And Sarah could find just enough energy to say, "I'm Sarah."

Sarah had never wondered what it would be like to tell the total truth. If asked, she would have said she had done it numerous times before. And it would have been a lie, as much to herself as to the person who had asked. Now, she understood this. Now, she wanted to try to tell the total truth.

They ended up where Sarah had been intending

to go all along—the bathroom off of the parental bedroom. Mom's bathroom, clearly, with its museum of perfume bottles, its royal-majesty mirror, and its hand towels embroidered with shells. With the party raging on, it was the quietest part of the apartment. Lindsay sat on the edge of the tub while Sarah put the seat cover down and sat on the toilet.

"What is it?" Lindsay asked.

"Can I really tell you?"

Lindsay nodded.

"I don't want to be here," Sarah said. "I don't really want to be anywhere I usually go. I have no idea where I want to be instead, but I know that I can't keep going to the same places. My friends have no idea who I am, and maybe I don't know who they are, either, but they live much more on the surface than I do. Is that awful to say? I don't mean it as an insult. They're the way they are and I'm the way I am. Neither way is better or worse. It's just that my way is better for me."

Lindsay didn't pass judgment. Instead she asked,

"So why did you come tonight?"

Sarah shook her head slowly. "Because I can usually trick myself into thinking I'm going to have a good time. It's like this social amnesia kicks in, and I forget how ugly I feel and how out of place I am and how miserable I'll be. It's amazing how you can convince yourself of something when you don't think you have any options."

I should be crying, Sarah thought. She was effectively erasing everything that was supposed to matter to her. What her friends thought. What the guys might think.

Lindsay heard what Sarah was saying and she knew: This was a girl who wanted to walk away. And who *would* walk away, even if it hurt. What Lindsay felt then wasn't the desire to walk away, too, but instead the desire to remain. She knew that Sarah's problems were not her own, even if she could understand where Sarah was coming from.

"I just don't want to be here," Sarah said again.

And Lindsay replied, "You should never be somewhere you truly don't want to be."

"Is it that simple?" Sarah asked.

And Lindsay said yes, it was that simple.

There is such freedom in learning you can leave.

★ ★ ★

Less than a mile away, Stewart Hall was sitting with his friend Phil in Tompkins Square Park. Later, they would each wonder whether being outdoors made them more susceptible to the night. The day hadn't been at all out of the ordinary; Stewart had gotten new headphones at Best Buy while Phil had worked on an English paper and had IM'd with a girl named Deborah who he'd met over the summer at camp. The conversation had been inconsequential; they often chatted about visiting each other, but they never did.

"So what's up?" Stewart asked. They'd just gotten to the park.

"Not much," Phil answered. "You?"

"Not much."

It was Stewart who'd called Phil, who'd said they should hang out. They usually met in the park, then saw who else came by.

"Not much?" Phil said.

"Yeah, not much."

Phil started thinking.

"And how are you?" he asked.

"What do you mean, how am I?"

"I mean, how are you?"

"Fine."

"Fine?"

"Yeah, fine."

"You tired?"

"Are you kidding?"

"No. You tired?"

"Hell yes, I'm tired. I'm always fucking tired."

Phil nodded. "You know what I wonder?"

"I have a feeling you're going to tell me."

"Yeah, I'm gonna tell you. I'm wondering, why are the answers to these questions always the same?"

"What questions?"

"You ask 'What's up?' I say 'Not much.' Then I ask 'What's up?' and you say 'Not much.' And if anyone asks how we're feeling, or how we're doing, we say, 'Fine.' And if someone asks if we're tired, we say of course we're tired. Because everyone is tired. There is not a single person we know who isn't tired. That's the only truthful answer of the three."

Normally, Stewart would just tell Phil to get his head out of his ass, but for some reason he went along with it. He was listening, which wasn't something he always did with Phil.

"But isn't 'not much' true?" he asked. "I mean, are you saying that something's up and I don't know about it?"

"I'm just saying that if nothing's up and we're all feeling fine, then why are we so tired all the time? *Something's* got to be happening." Phil stood up from the bench. "We can't all be doing nothing, right?"

"I'm not saying 'nothing,'" Stewart pointed out. "I'm saying 'not much.'"

But Phil was already heading somewhere. Since the weather was so perfect, there were a lot of people in the park, even long after sunset, well into the night.

"Where are you going?" Stewart asked. Then, not getting an answer, he followed.

There were two girls from the neighborhood sitting on a bench about twenty feet away. Tamika and Danika, or something like that.

"What's up?" Phil said to them.

"Not much," they responded.

He nodded and moved on to the next bench. A homeless guy who smelled like bad cheese.

"What's up?" Phil asked.

"Not much," the guy said.

Third bench. A poet type with a black notebook on his lap, pen poised for words that he clearly sensed were on the way.

"What's up?" Phil asked.

The poet looked up thoughtfully from his poetry daze.

"Not much," he replied. "Not much at all."

Stewart could sense his friend getting more and more frustrated. But still, he wasn't expecting what happened next.

They saw a few members of their group—

Mateo, Ben, Miranda—ahead.

"Hey, man, I called you!" Mateo yelled out when he saw them coming.

"Hey!" Phil yelled back. Then, when they were closer, he asked it: "What's up?"

And Mateo said, "Not much."

Next, Phil asked Ben, and Ben said, "Not much." Then Miranda, and she said it too.

"That's not true!" he yelled. "We're all so full of shit—'not much not much not much.' Mateo, *something* has to be up. Ben, I know there's something going on in that head of yours. Miranda, why don't you just come right out and say it?"

Something clicked into place then. Was it the way Phil said it? Or was it the light or the scent in the air that opened them up? Or maybe they were just tired of not really answering. Whatever the cause, Stewart could actually see the change—the way Phil's question was suddenly a real question, not just something to say.

"You want to know what's up?" Miranda asked. "You really want to know?"

Phil nodded.

"Well, I'll tell you," she said. "I'm here with Mateo and Ben, right? But I'm also on the lookout for my brother, because he's been acting weird lately, and I think he might be coming to the park to get some. I mean, we've hardly seen him in the past few weeks, and when he's home, he'll just lock the door and do whatever behind it. The other night, we were both brushing our teeth at the same time, and I tried to ask him what was going on, but he just looked at me like I was some girl renting a room from his parents, and he said nothing was going on. Nothing at all. I just thought he was being a jerk, but then when he was leaving, he tells me not to worry. And I'm thinking, if there's nothing to worry about, then why is he telling me not to worry? I know who he hangs out with, and they're not a problem, but suddenly I'm wondering if he's hanging out with someone else I don't know about, or if he's gotten into trouble. I mean, I know he's done some shit in the past, but it's always been under control. He's got his friend Mike, who keeps him in line. But it's not like I can call Mike and ask him what's going on—Darius would knock me in the head if he knew I did that. So I'm just trying to see what I can see, you know? Darius likes to come to the park and do his thing. So maybe I'll catch him at it."

"How 'bout you?" Phil asked, turning to Mateo. "What's up?"

"I'm not over Deena," he said. "You *know* that's what's up."

"You hoping to see her?" Miranda asked.

"I'm always hoping to see her. Even when I'm all like *fuck hope*, I'm still hoping."

"And you, Ben?" Phil asked. "What's up?"

"Just had to get out of my house, man. Being there makes me feel like I'm living a murder, you know?"

Phil didn't know. None of them knew. Ben never talked about home.

Phil thought: We talk all the time about people opening up, as if it's some kind of physical unfolding. But the only thing that can open us up to another person is words. Words on the inside, telling us to do the things we're most afraid to do. Words on the outside, sharing what's really going on.

Sometimes all we need is a little attention to open up.

★ ★ ★

People kept knocking on the bathroom door, but Sarah and Lindsay didn't feel too guilty about staying locked inside; they knew there were at least two other bathrooms in the apartment. People could deal.

Then there came a knock that was less insistent, more of a question than a statement.

A voice followed it.

"Sarah, you in there? It's me, Ashley."

Lindsay watched Sarah, wondering what she was going to do.

Sarah didn't seem to be surprised at being found, or even that worried.

"What is it, Ashley?" she asked through the door.

"I was just looking for you. Are you okay? You've

been gone for a long time."

Sarah noticed the *I*—Ashley was almost never an *I*. This had to mean that Amanda had found her guy and left Ashley to the wolves.

Sarah sighed. Had she really thought her life wouldn't be able to find her? Did she really think it would get distracted and not notice she was gone? She looked to Lindsay, silently asking if it was okay for her to open the door, to let the interloper in. Lindsay nodded; she knew from experience that even though it was important to hide away in the bathroom when you needed to, it was equally important to leave it eventually.

Ashley looked stupidly confused when the door finally opened and she found two girls inside. Had Sarah and this girl been making out? Was Sarah a *lesbian*? Ashley couldn't understand how a bathroom could be used for anything other than making out or, well, going to the bathroom. Ashley wasn't perceptive so much as receptive; she needed someone to explain things to her. And Amanda was too busy flirting with Greg to be there.

Sarah said, "Ashley, this is Lindsay. Lindsay, Ashley."

This new girl held out her hand, and Ashley wondered if she'd washed it. After either making out with Sarah or going to the bathroom. Whichever.

It looked clean, so she shook it. Then she asked Sarah what she was doing.

"Just talking," Sarah said. "I needed to get away."

Get away? Ashley was confused. They'd only been here for a half hour or so. Which was long for being in the bathroom, but pretty short for being at a party.

The next possible explanation that came into her head was that Sarah had gotten her period and Lindsay had given her a tampon. Although that didn't explain why Lindsay was in the bathroom with Sarah, or why Sarah hadn't asked Ashley or Amanda for a tampon. Not that Ashley or Amanda would have had one; this one time, Amanda's purse fell open when she was with a boy and the tampons had fallen in his lap, and Amanda had been so mortified that she said they would just have to rely on scamming them off other girls from now on. Ashley had actually sent this story in anonymously to a teen magazine's embarrassing moments column, but they hadn't printed it.

Sarah could not for the life of her figure out what was going on in Ashley's head. More than anything, she wanted Ashley to go back to the party and leave her and Lindsay alone again. Sarah knew she should never have opened the door. Now there'd be no closing it again.

"There you are," a male voice said. A not-as-cute-as-his-clothes indie-rock boy was shouldering into the doorway, looking at Lindsay. "I totally lost you."

Lindsay was happy to see Jimm, only not right now. This girl needed her more than he did. At least until she left the party.

"Jimm, Sarah. Sarah, Jimm," Lindsay introduced. "And . . . I'm sorry, I've already forgotten your name."

"Ashley."

"Jimm, Ashley. Ashley, Jimm."

The presence of a boy made Ashley stop thinking too much, especially since he was clearly with Lindsay, and therefore Lindsay wasn't a lesbian. Not that Ashley minded lesbians. She would just be hurt if Sarah had been one all along and hadn't told her and Amanda.

On other nights, Sarah would have given in. She would have asked Ashley where Amanda was, and they would have headed to that general vicinity together, to chaperone her flirtation and provide interruption if it was needed. She would have let Amanda's guy introduce her to the guy she was supposed to fall for tonight, and maybe she would have been so bored that she would have fallen for him. Or at least pretended to, if he was pitiable enough. But not tonight.

"I'm going to go," Sarah told Ashley.

"But we just got here!" Ashley replied.

"I'm going to go," Sarah repeated, this time to Lindsay.

"You should," Lindsay told her. "Go do something you want to do."

"I just want to wander," Sarah said.

"Then wander."

"C'mon, Sarah," Ashley said. And Sarah felt bad, because she knew if Amanda was in the boy zone, Ashley was going to be a barflower for the rest of the night.

"Do you want to come with me?" she asked.

Ashley shook her head. "Is it cramps?" she whispered.

Sarah decided to avoid the polite lie.

"I don't belong here," she said. "I'd rather be doing something else. So I'm going to do something else."

Ashley took it personally, even though Sarah had asked her along.

"Are you mad at me?" she asked.

And Sarah thought, *Well, I wasn't until you said that.*

Lindsay was scribbling her phone number on the back of a receipt.

"Call me when you get there," she said, passing the paper over.

"I will," Sarah said, and hugged Lindsay good-bye. Then she did the same to Ashley, who was still confused.

As Sarah pushed forward into the crowded hallways, a strange grace filled her. Instead of being sick of all the people around her, she recognized that many of them were actually having fun. This crowded, loud, playerful atmosphere was the right kind for them.

She laughed when she got to the door and realized she didn't have her coat. Then she plunged back in, seeing Amanda out of the corner of her eye as she passed the living room. Amanda was in firm girl-grasp of her target guy's arm. Her peripheral vision was turned off, so Sarah could slide by, retrieve her coat from underneath a guy in the third stage of passing out, then head back to the door.

As soon as she was out of the apartment, she felt free.

It didn't matter that she had nowhere to go. *Nowhere to go* was the perfect destination.

While Mateo, Miranda, Ben, and Stewart talked about what was going on with them, Phil sneaked away. He wasn't done with his questions. There was still some kind of answer he was looking for, but he hadn't found it yet.

He saw two guys sitting on a bench, both about his age, probably from Stuy or Bronx Science or one of the other smart high schools. They were clearly with each other, but they weren't really talking. It reminded Phil a little of him and Stewart, how some nights they'd sit around for hours and wait for something to happen instead of making it happen themselves.

One of the guys was lost in thought, and Phil could see how that would happen on a night like tonight. The second guy looked at Phil strangely as he headed over.

"Hey," Phil said to the guy who seemed to be paying attention. "What's up?"

"We don't want any drugs," the guy replied. "Sorry."

Damn, Phil thought. *Do I look like a dealer?*

He laughed. "I'm not selling drugs. Just coming by, saying what's up."

"Oh," the guy said. He didn't seem to know what to do with that. He wasn't exactly apologizing. Almost as an afterthought, he added, "Not much really going on."

The quiet guy looked up now. No longer lost in thought, because clearly there was one thought that had found him and was taking hold. It was hurting him.

"What's up?" Phil asked him.

"You're not the person I should be telling," the boy replied.

"Fair enough," Phil said. "Fair enough."

Suddenly he felt out of place, self-conscious. Why was he talking to strangers? What was he trying to find?

But there was something in that quiet boy's eyes.

"Say it," Phil told him. "Not to me. But to whoever you need to say it to."

"Thanks for your advice," the louder guy said sarcastically.

"See you," Phil said. He saw a girl he knew, Isabel, coming into the park. He wanted to get to her before she saw the others.

"What's up?" he called out to her, leaving the two guys on their bench.

"Oh, it's all the same," she said, coming over for a hug. "You know."

"What do I know?" Phil asked. "Remind me."

★ ★ ★

"What was that about?" Simon asked. Even if he'd been sarcastic with the guy who'd come over, the sarcasm was diluted now by a simple confusion.

"He was just being friendly," Leo replied. "Remember friendly?"

They were both in a bad mood, and Simon wasn't sure why. Leo had been weird all night. Simon had been friends with him long enough to know what these moods were like, and how to get through them. But usually he also had a clue about what had caused them—Leo knowing he had to dump his boyfriend, Leo feeling he was fucking up his chances at a good school, Leo feeling overwhelmed by his parents' expectations and his feeling that his writing was never going to be any good. Simon knew these things because he and Leo talked about them. But tonight: nothing. At dinner they'd volleyed between trivia and silence. Normally Simon might not have even noticed. But tonight he did, and Leo's bad mood started to put him in his own bad mood. Maybe it would have been a good thing if the guy *had* been selling drugs. It would've been something to do.

"I love you."

Simon had been zoning out, but he heard it. So quiet, but unmistakable. He turned to Leo.

"What?"

"Nothing."

"No. Tell me."

Leo sighed. The saddest, deepest sigh. "I said 'I love you.'"

"To who?"

"To you."

Simon didn't know where this was coming from. "Well, I love you, too," he said.

"No, not like that, Simon. I mean, I really love you."

Simon was about to respond, but before he could, Leo went on.

"You have no idea how many times I've told you. I can't believe you finally heard. I have been saying 'I love you' to you for years. *Years*. Sometimes when you're asleep on the subway and I'm sitting next to you. Sometimes if the music's really loud. Or if we're at the movies and you're not paying attention to me. I'll be watching you watching the screen, and I'll say it really softly, and I've always felt that if you were meant to hear it, then you'd hear it. I have been in love with you for years, Simon, and it's become too heavy. I can't do it anymore. I know it's ridiculous and I know this is going to be a disaster, but you have to understand it's been a disaster for me to try to keep it inside, only letting it out in all of these *I love you*s that you never hear. I know you're going to be kind to me, because that's what you do. I know you're going to say that we're friends, and that it's about friendship, but you have no idea how many times I've watched you, how many times I've had fierce arguments with myself about you. I always told you the truth when you weren't listening—and now you're listening, and it scares the hell out of me. I know this will change everything, and it will probably screw it all up, but I have lived with this so long, Simon, and I just can't do it alone anymore. I have to tell someone, and that someone needs to be you. That guy—that guy asked, 'What's up?' And I realized that the answer to the question was 'I love Simon.' Whether you lean over and kiss me—which I know isn't going to happen—or whether you push me away and tell me you don't want to see me again—which I'm pretty sure isn't going to happen either—I just need something to happen. I can't keep having the same feelings over and over again in secret. Because if you hold something inside long enough, you start to hate it. And I don't want to hate you. The opposite, really. I love you, you see. I love you."

"But Leo—" Simon began.

"No," Leo interrupted. "Please don't start with a *but . . .*"

Sarah couldn't figure out what was happening in the city that night. As she wandered, she was witnessing the strangest things. Shopkeepers walking out of stores, leaving them unlocked, wandering off with their aprons still on. Waiters walking away with their order pads still in their waistbands, taking out cell phones and saying, "I need to see you now." There were painful, aching fights in the streets—not between strangers, but among friends or lovers or people trying to be either, the truth suddenly so plain to see. People were clutching at photographs, searching through purses for the love notes they could never throw out. Love had suddenly become an active verb—prodded, confessed, kissed into words. There were no innocent bystanders, because how could you see this and not think of the person who love always made you think about? Or you felt the absence of that person. Or, like Sarah, you felt the absence of the absence. Walking through the honest chaos, she felt moved but untouched. *I am myself*, she thought. *I am myself*. And that was okay. That was fine. That was what she wanted.

★ ★ ★

"What's up?" Phil asked.

"My mother is dying and I don't know what to do."

"What's up?"

"I'm a fake. And I'm not going to get away with it."

"What's up?"

"It's a beautiful night, don't you think?"

"What's up?"

"Phil, I haven't seen you in two or three months. And I'm not ready to forgive you for that."

"What's up?"

"The opposite of down?"

"What's up?"

"I'm afraid of this park. Bad things happen in this park."

"What's up?"

"I need to eat."

"What's up?"

"I feel guilty because I forget about the war."

"What's up?"

"I just want to be happy, and I don't know if that will ever happen."

"What's up?"

"It's getting late, isn't it? I feel like it's getting late."

★ ★ ★

But Leo, Simon thought, *I will never love you like that.*

★ ★ ★

Sarah was not used to being up so late. The city, she felt, had entered its vulnerable hours, not quite awake and not quite asleep, not quite loud but unable to be silent, the line blurring between what was thought and what was said.

She thought briefly of Ashley and Amanda, that old life that would probably still be hers in the morning. She wondered if Lindsay was still at the party, or if she had gone home. Maybe she would be a new part of the old life. Maybe the old life could have new parts.

The streets were getting less and less crowded, as people took their confessions indoors. Walking through the East Village, Sarah could see that many lights were still on, and even if they were off, it didn't necessarily mean that the people inside were asleep. Murmurs and moans, conversations and truths in many forms seeped through the walls and into the streets. Sarah could hear some of the shouting coming from the street-level apartments—*"You never loved me!" "This is what I want you to do." "You are too good for me, and I've always known it."* She did not stop to listen. These things had everything to do with the night, but nothing to do with her.

When the streets had been more crowded, Sarah had been overwhelmed by the immensity of humanity, how many of us there are and how little we can affect. Now, with the streets emptying out, she was struck by a different kind of immensity— the immensity of space and building, the immensity of all that's around us. It didn't make her feel inconsequential, as it normally might. Instead, she found some comfort in the immensity. It guaranteed that she could always wander. And it also guaranteed that she'd never have to wander too far.

She followed Eighth Street until she got to the park. It, too, was emptying out. People looked exhausted from speaking, but glad about what had been said. On one bench, two guys held on to each other, one of them clasping, the other one trying to comfort. On another bench, a young woman cried silently, shaking her head in disbelief. But not everyone was sad or longing. Other couples kissed under lamplight—some extending the kiss beneath their clothing. Sarah saw one guy watching it all, looking more exhausted than most. She'd had no desire to talk to anyone for hours, ever since she'd left Lindsay. But now the impulse returned. As she walked over, he looked up at her. He didn't say anything until she'd arrived.

"What's up?" he asked.

"Not much," she said. "And everything."

Because wasn't that the truth of it? In terms of the immensities, nothing much was happening to Sarah. But on her own terms, things were.

"What's up with you?" she asked back.

It was the first time the whole night that a stranger had offered Phil this. And now that it had been asked, he realized it was what he had been waiting for. It was what he needed. And he couldn't figure out how to respond.

"I'd like to be able to give you an answer," he said. "I'd like to know."

He began to tell her everything that had happened that night—all the people he'd asked, all the answers he'd received. Stewart and the others were long gone; he was the only one of his friends left in the park. It was as if he had lost something here, and he had to find it before he could leave. But he wasn't sure what it was, or what it looked like.

"It's a strange night," Sarah said. Then she told Phil about the party, about leaving, about wandering. She told him about the vulnerable hours, even as the sky started to tinge with lightness.

"It's loneliness," he said. "These hours bring out the loneliness."

"I'm not sure," Sarah told him. "I used to think it was loneliness, when I thought about it at all. But maybe it's just the fear of loneliness. I think that makes us more vulnerable. But tonight I don't mind being alone. If you let go of everyone else, it's amazing what you can see."

"And who you can meet," Phil added.

Hours ago, Sarah would have thought this was a flirtation. But now it was just an observation. A late-night, early-morning observation in the middle of an empty park and a full city.

"I'm Sarah," she said, offering her hand.

"I'm Phil," he said, taking it.

"I'll be here tomorrow at sunset."

"In that case, so will I."

And with that, they parted. Because Sarah wanted her wandering to end at home. Because she wanted to start the new part of her old life. Because she realized now: If you can conquer the vulnerable hours, you can allow yourself to be yourself, to go forward. You breathe in the night air, and it sustains you.

David Levithan is the critically acclaimed author of *Boy Meets Boy*; *The Realm of Possibility*; *Are We There Yet*; *Marly's Ghost*; *Wide Awake*; *How They Met, and Other Stories*; and (with Rachel Cohn) *Nick and Norah's Infinite Playlist* and *Naomi and Ely's No Kiss List*. He's won Lambda Literary Awards for *Boy Meets Boy* and *The Full Spectrum* (edited with Billy Merrell), and his books have appeared on ALA's Best Books for Young Adults list in 2004, 2005, 2006, and 2007. He is also the founding editor of PUSH, an imprint dedicated to new authors and new voices, and teaches in the New School's MFA program. You can visit him online at www.davidlevithan.com. Just don't expect him to respond to emails late at night—he barely managed to stay up all night when he was in college, and that was some time ago.

ORANGE
ALERT

Patricia McCormick

Like pretty much everyone else in this middle-of-nowhere town, I got my learner's permit exactly six months before my sixteenth birthday. Unlike everyone else, though, I taught myself to drive.

At first, I just sat in the driver's seat of my mom's old car after school. I wouldn't even put the key in the ignition. I'd just go out front where the car was parked next to the curb and put my hands on the wheel in the ten o'clock and two o'clock positions like it says in the driver's ed manual. I pretended I was breezing down the highway, keeping a light but steady pressure on the accelerator, always ready to tap the brake if I needed to. I also practiced changing lanes, checking the rearview mirror, then the side view, then snapping the turn signal down. Eventually I worked up to imaginary three-point turns, even throwing my arm over the back of the passenger seat as I backed up, the way cops do on TV.

But I always made sure I was out of the car and inside doing my homework by the time Ed, my stepfather, got home at five thirty. The last thing I needed was for him to see how badly I wanted to learn.

★ ★ ★

A couple months ago, before I turned fifteen and a half, I asked Ed to teach me. I said everyone else's parents were letting their kids practice driving before they got their permits.

"Well, young lady," he said, not looking up from his paper, "everyone else's parents are breaking the law."

I blew out a little huff of air with my bottom lip.

Ed set the paper down. Slowly.

"You have a problem with that?" He peered over the paper at me, then at my chest. I wrapped my arms around myself and shook my head.

"Pardon me?"

"Huh-uh."

"Huh-uh?" He said this in a high-pitched girl's voice that was supposed to be an imitation of mine.

"No," I said.

"No, what?"

"No, sir."

Ed was in the Army. He wore a tan uniform to work every day, but all he did was scuttle around on a stool on wheels and grab file folders off a machine that looked like a giant Ferris wheel. If you were really good at it, like Ed, you could "retrieve" or "archive" twelve files a minute. It was only the file room at the Army Depot in Nowheresville, USA, but Ed made it sound like he, personally, was the secret weapon in the war on terror. His reflexes, he says, are always on Orange Alert.

"Besides," he said, "you'd probably kill us both."

★★★

My mom would shake her head when I came in after one of my driving lessons. "If he catches you . . . " Then she would just stop and shrug, turning her palms up toward the ceiling like there was nothing she could do about it.

"He won't," I'd say.

Up until last year my mom used to drive. But after we moved into Ed's house and she quit her hair-cutting job at the Mane Event so she could be a stay-at-home wife like Ed wanted her to be, she lets him do the driving. "It makes him feel important," she says.

"What's your hurry, anyway?" my mom said. She was standing at the sink peeling a carrot and wearing her robe and slippers even though it was almost four o'clock. Lately, she didn't take her shower until right before Ed got home, since he said he liked her to be "fresh" when he came in the door. "You can't even take the driving test for another six months."

I shrugged. I didn't honestly know what my hurry was. I just knew that whenever I pictured myself the way I wanted to be, I pictured myself behind the wheel of a car.

★ ★ ★

Eventually I threw in dangerous weather conditions, reckless drivers, and assorted emergencies—toddlers darting into the street to chase after balls, trees falling on rain-slicked highways, tire blowouts, and black ice—to add excitement and variety to my curbside driving lessons. I thrilled myself by how calm and quick-witted I was—pumping the brakes, not slamming them; steering into the spin, not jerking the wheel in the opposite direction—when confronted with these unanticipated driving challenges.

One day I was so involved in passing an eighteen-wheeler in a hailstorm that I didn't realize that Ed had come home. It wasn't until I looked in the rearview mirror to make sure I could see the truck's headlights in my right sideview mirror before I changed lanes that I saw Ed standing behind the car, his hands in his pockets, like he'd been there all day just waiting for me to notice him.

My first impulse was to lock the car door the

way my mom used to do when we had to drive in the city. But when I realized the window was open, I just sat there with my arms folded across my chest.

Ed strolled slowly around to the driver's side and leaned in the window. He got so close, I could see the pores on his nose. "Having fun?"

There was no right answer to this question. If I said yes, Ed would make fun of me. If I said no, he'd make fun of me.

"I guess."

"You *guess*?"

I reached for the door handle and pushed. Nothing happened. Ed had me pinned inside, his arm braced against the door. I glanced across the front seat at the passenger-side door. It seemed too far away to attempt. "Let me out, Ed." I meant it to sound tough, but my voice came out puny and babyish.

"You want to drive," he said. "So drive."

I didn't move.

"C'mon," he said. "I'm waiting."

I rammed the car door with my shoulder. It didn't budge.

"What's the matter?" Ed said.

I stared straight ahead out the windshield.

"What's the matter?" he said again, in a fake-sympathetic voice. "Don't tell me you can't."

That's exactly what Ed wanted—for me to tell him that I couldn't, that I didn't know how, that I was just a stupid kid playing make-believe.

I looked away. Then I looked right at him. "I can't."

Ed smacked his hand against his forehead—his imitation of someone just figuring out something obvious. "Oh, that's right," he said. "I forgot. You *can't*."

Then Ed made a big display of opening the car door for me like I was a guest or something. As I got out, his hand snaked across my waist and landed on the back pocket of my jeans. He grabbed hold of my butt and gave it a squeeze.

I spun around and glared at him.

But by then his hands were sticking up in the air,

his face all innocent like nothing had happened. He wiggled his fingers back and forth. "Orange Alert, kid."

I stomped across the yard.

"Where do you think you're going?" he said.

"Nowhere."

He laughed. "That's exactly where you're going. Nowhere."

★ ★ ★

For the next few days, I skipped my driving lessons. I went up to my room right after school and changed into shorts and a tank top, since Ed says we can't turn on the air conditioner until after Memorial Day even though it's already about a hundred degrees. Every day at exactly four thirty my mom would start showering and making herself "fresh" for dinner, and every day at five thirty-five, Ed slammed the front door and shouted, "Honeys, I'm home." And every day I jacked up the volume on my iPod and went back to doing whatever it was I was doing.

One day I was picking the polish off my nails

when Ed poked his head into my room and waited for me to pay attention to him. I sighed, pulled out one of the earbuds, and waited to hear what he had to say that was so important.

He made a serious face. "Been meaning to ask you," he said. "What kinda mileage you getting on that car?" Then he threw his head back and laughed like this was the funniest thing anyone had ever said.

I put my earbud back in and jacked the volume up some more, but Ed was still standing there, looking at me the way a dog looks at a steak on the grill. So I grabbed my sweatshirt and put it on, even though it was probably 112 degrees by now. Ed shook his head and left.

A couple of days later at dinner, Ed told us about a new guy at work. "This kid is so slow," Ed said, "he can only do about two retrievals a minute. Two point five tops." He shook his head, like this guy was clearly a major threat to homeland security.

My mom beamed at Ed, the way she used to

beam at Tony and Jim and Ken and all the other guys who were supposed to be the One—until Tony and Jim and Ken and all the others met somebody a little younger, a little prettier. She cleared her throat like she had an important announcement to make.

"I made a lemon meringue pie today," she said.

Ed rolled his eyes.

"Now, don't be like that, honey," she said. "I did like you said. I waited to whip the meringue this time, so it's just the way you like it."

Ed gave her an I'll-believe-it-when-I-see-it look.

"Now, *you* just relax," she said to Ed. "And *you* clear the table," she said to me. "I'll be back in a jiffy."

I got up and started stacking the plates and wondering when exactly my mom turned into someone who spent her afternoons in a robe and slippers making lemon meringue pies and using words like *jiffy*. I scraped all the leftover pork-chop bones onto one plate, stacked the others underneath, then piled the forks and knives on top. I picked the whole stack of dishes up with one hand, took the ketchup bottle and stuck it between my elbow and my ribs, and grabbed my milk glass with my free hand. It was what Ed called a lazy man's load. But it meant that I'd have to make one less trip to the kitchen and back, one less chance for Ed to look at me the way he does when my mom's not around.

I was just about to walk out when Ed reached over and put the salad bowl on top of the pile of plates in my hand. It was the good salad bowl, the one that used to belong to my grandma, and I could see right away that if I took a step, it would fall. He smirked at me as the whir of the mixer came from the kitchen. "What's your hurry?" he said.

Slowly, I set the stack of dishes back down on the table, balancing the whole thing carefully so the salad bowl wouldn't crash to the floor. Before I could rearrange the load, Ed was on his feet. He grabbed me by the shoulders and pulled me toward him. My arms were pinned against my sides and I could smell the leftover dinner on his breath as his mouth came toward mine. I jerked my head to the side. The mixer shut off and I could hear my mom humming in the kitchen. I squirmed and Ed tightened his grip. He whispered in my ear. "One of these nights . . ." He dug his fingers into my arms. "Just you wait," he said. Then he let go, just as my mom walked in holding the pie.

"What are you doing?" Her expression went from proud to confused.

Ed pointed to the salad bowl perched on top of the dinner dishes. "Just teaching the kid a thing or two," he said. He picked the bowl up and handed it to me. "You understand me?"

I clenched my teeth together and nodded.

★ ★ ★

That night, after my mom and Ed were asleep, I started my real driving lessons. I waited until I heard the TV go off in their room. I counted to a hundred ten times, then another ten times, then I slipped out of my room. I tiptoed downstairs to the kitchen, lifted the key to my mom's car off the hook, and let myself out of the house. It was an old car, the kind without an alarm, so all I had to do was slip the key in the lock and ease the door open little by little. I slid into the driver's seat and released the emergency brake. At first nothing happened. Then the car started rolling, ever so slowly, down the hill. It picked up speed as I passed the next-door neighbor's house. I coasted past their house, then the next one, then the next one. The only sound was a slight *shhh* of the tires gliding over the pavement.

At the bottom of the hill there was a stop sign. I pressed on the brake and the car came to a complete and perfect halt. I sat there for a minute under the glow of a streetlight and considered what to do next. It was nearly one in the morning. I was in my pajama pants, a T-shirt, and slippers. Behind the wheel of a car. I had to bite my lip to keep from laughing out loud. I turned the key in the ignition. The car came to life and I knew what to do next.

I looked right, then left, put on my turn signal,

and turned the steering wheel a few degrees to the left. I took my foot off the brake, applied a light but steady pressure to the accelerator, and proceeded up Pennbrook Street. I turned left again on Meadowview, then left again, until I found myself back at the top of my own street. I rounded the corner, then shut off the motor two mailboxes before ours and let the car coast, applying the brakes expertly, until it came to rest back at the curb in front of the house exactly where it had been only a few minutes earlier.

I slid out of the driver's seat, inched the door shut, locked it, and slipped back inside the house without making a sound. When I got back to my room, I was suddenly so tired that I fell asleep instantly and didn't wake up until the alarm went off the next morning.

★ ★ ★

Ed looked smaller somehow when I came down for breakfast. I also noticed, as I carried my bowl of cereal past him while he sat reading the paper and muttering about the idiots running this country, that his hair was thinning near the back of his head where he couldn't see.

★ ★ ★

I did the same thing the next night. Except that this time I got dressed and went as far as the end of our development. The next night I took the car out on the highway. It was then that I realized that despite what adults want you to think when they yell at you and tell you shut up so they can concentrate, driving just isn't that hard. I drove up the highway to the next exit, turned around, and came back. On the way back, I turned the radio up all the way, rolled down the window, and cruised along with one arm out the window and the other one resting lightly on the steering wheel. As I crossed the front yard when I got back home, my joints felt loose, like they were full of air. There was only one way to describe this feeling: powerful.

★ ★ ★

The next night, I was cruising along the highway, not exactly awake or asleep, when I saw an exit for a town I didn't recognize. The middle-of-the-night DJ came on, saying that he was going to "make way for the morning crew." I had to really push it on the way back—the speedometer gave a little shudder when it hit eighty-five—to get home before Ed got up.

★ ★ ★

Ed looked at me sort of suspiciously when I sat down at the table for breakfast.

"Get a good night's sleep?" he asked, stabbing a piece of sausage.

I shrugged and waited for him to make me say that yes, I'd gotten a good night's sleep. Sir.

But he just kept studying me. "You sure you slept okay?" he asked.

I said I was sure.

"'Cause you look a little tired."

I swallowed. "I'm fine."

That's when I felt Ed's hand on my thigh. "I know how you girls need your beauty sleep," he said.

By the time my mom came over to refill Ed's mug, his hands were folded on the table in front of him.

He winked at me as she walked away to put the

coffeepot back on the counter. "Orange Alert," he said. "Always on Orange Alert."

★ ★ ★

That night I figured I should probably take a break from my driving lessons. I couldn't sleep after I heard the TV go off in my mom and Ed's room, though, so I was lying in bed, counting to a hundred for the tenth time, when I heard the sound of a floorboard creaking in their room. I held perfectly still. Then came another creak. I didn't wait to hear more. I jumped out of bed, ran to the kitchen, grabbed the keys off the hook, and slipped out the door.

★ ★ ★

It wasn't until I was way past the turnoff for the highway that I realized I'd gone too far. I was on a windy country road that seemed to just go on and on, past dairy farms and cornfields and more dairy farms and more cornfields. I knew vaguely that I was lost, that I should turn around, but I kept going. It was a whole new driving challenge, nothing like what I used to dream up in my curbside driving lessons. The point was simply to go and go and go, to inch the speedometer up so high it shivered, to hit the accelerator at the crest of a hill so that the car would actually leave the road for one long, beautiful second and then hit the pavement with a stomach-dropping scrape.

It wasn't until the yellow line in the middle of the road started to blur, then fracture into a million tiny pieces, that I realized I'd finally encountered the one driving challenge I couldn't handle—the tears that seemed to be pooling in my eyes no matter how hard I tried to blink them back. The yellow line swam before my eyes. The road turned to fog. The car rounded a curve and the back tires spun out with a screech.

I slammed on the brake. The car spun sideways, then swung sickeningly in the other direction. There was a far-off *thunk*, then a small crumpling noise, like the sound of a soda can being flattened. The car rocked to a halt. I seemed to have had nothing to do with this. It had simply stopped. I opened the door, got out, and took in the sight of the car, sitting at the side of the road at a weird angle. The back door was dented. I understood then that I had hit a fence post; it was leaning into the road, straining on the barbed wire that connected it to the rest of the fence. But everything else—including me—was fine.

I got back in, executed a perfect three-point turn, and headed home.

★ ★ ★

It was still dark when I got to the top of our street, but I could see Ed standing by the curb in his pajamas, his hands on his hips. I didn't have to think about what to do.

I didn't turn off the motor two mailboxes before ours like I normally did.

I kept my foot on the gas.

I didn't speed up. I didn't slow down. I aimed straight for Ed.

As I got close, I could see that he was smirking. When I got a little closer, he started to look confused. His mouth was stalled in midsmirk, but his eyebrows were scrunched together the way they did when he couldn't work the computer.

As I got even closer, I saw what I wanted to see: Ed was scared.

He jumped out of the way at the last minute, tripping over the curb and landing face-first on grass. Which means neither of us will know what I would've done if he hadn't.

But I think we both knew then that Ed wouldn't be bothering me anymore.

I stopped the car a few feet past where he was lying on the grass, switched off the ignition, and got out.

I turned and looked at him before heading back inside. "Orange Alert, Ed," I said. "You better be on Orange Alert."

TARA SCROI

Patricia McCormick has won numerous awards for her novels *Cut*, *My Brother's Keeper*, and *Sold*, which was a National Book Award nominee and was named by *Publishers Weekly* as one of the 100 Best Books of 2006. Her writing has been described by *VOYA* as "breathtaking in both its simplicity and attention to detail . . . stunning." She lives in New York City with her family. You can visit her online at www.pattymccormick.com.

SUPERMAN
IS DEAD

Sarah Weeks

No way. I'm not telling you what I did. You'll copy it," I say, putting my feet up on the coffee table and grabbing a throw pillow off the end of the couch to jam behind my neck. "I will tell you this, though: I totally rocked it."

The assignment is for AP English. Ms. Shaw gave us all the same photograph of a woman lying on her side in a lawn chair. There's a man sitting beside her, but all you see of him are his hands and the cuffs of his white dress shirt. The woman's back is to the camera, and in between the index and middle fingers of his right hand the man holds a lit cigarette. The assignment is to write a story about what we think was happening when the shutter clicked. Right up my alley.

"Come on," says Nick. "I won't steal your idea—I just want to hear what you did. It's ten o' clock already and I got nothing here. I need a jump start. Inspiration."

"Not my problem, man."

"Go ahead, be like that. But when you have to do the chem lab for tomorrow, don't be calling me to whine about how hard it is."

"Fine. I'll read it to you. But you have to promise—"

"Jeez, Brian, relax, will you? I'm not going to steal your stupid idea."

"*Brian?*" my little brother calls me from the other room. I ignore him.

"I don't have a title yet," I say.

"Brian!" my brother calls again.

"I'm on the phone!" I yell back.

"Babysitting?" asks Nick.

"Yeah. My mom's at some conference in Westchester. She's not coming back into the city until tomorrow afternoon."

"Wow," says Nick. "I can't believe she's letting you stay there alone overnight. Isn't she worried you're going to, like, party or something?"

"I'm not alone, remember? And Elsie's coming in the morning."

Elsie is Joe's babysitter. She was supposed to come and spend the night with us while my mother was at her conference, but at the last minute her own kid got sick and Elsie couldn't come. So my mother said she'd give me a hundred bucks to stay with Joe. Included in that price was a promise not to tell my father that she'd left us alone without an adult in the house.

"I'd never hear the end of it," she said.

My parents are divorced—the kind of divorced where they can't stand to be in the same room together or talk on the phone without having a huge fight. I can remember when they used to like each other. That was before Joe was born, and before my father met Brenda. She's my stepmother now, and Mom and I both hate her guts.

"You going to read it to me or what?" asks Nick. I read.

A little girl stood at the window looking down into the backyard.

"Mommy?" she called.

No answer. The sound of running water came from the kitchen. The girl called again, louder this time.

"Mommy?"

The water went off.

"Brittany-Michelle, how many times I gotta tell you? Don't yell if you want Mommy. Come to where I'm at."

"Mommy?"

An audible exhalation.

"I'm in the kitchen."

"Wait a second, back up," Nick interrupts. "An audible *huh*?"

"Audible exhalation," I tell him.

"What the heck is that?"

"Like a sigh."

"Where'd you get that from, thesaurus?"

"No. I made it up."

"No wonder Ms. Shaw loves you. *Audible exhalation.* Jeez."

"Do you want to hear this thing or not?" I say.

"Read," says Nick.

The girl and her mother had moved into the apartment the day before. Two hundred and fifty dollars a month. Three rooms over the garage. Wall-to-wall shag carpet, faded plaid curtains, fake walnut paneling. You could tell from the smell that a cat had lived there at some point. A double mattress lay on the floor, a tangle of sheets and blankets mounded up in the middle. The only other furniture in the room was a big TV, which sat on a cardboard box in the corner. There was a cartoon show on—a cat and a mouse chasing each other around with huge mallets. The little girl had her back to the TV. She was looking out the window into the yard where the new landlady, Mrs. Androtti, lay half naked in a lawnchair. There was a man sitting beside her. A minute ago his hands had been wrapped around the landlady's neck. Now he'd taken off his dark suit jacket and hung it over the back of his chair, and he was calmly smoking a cigarette.

"Brian, something's wrong with Superman."

My brother is standing in front of me with his arms crossed over his chest, his big blue eyes round with worry.

"I'm busy, Joe," I tell him.

He closes his eyes and squeezes out two fat tears, which catch in his lashes for a second, then drag race down his pale cheeks.

"What are you talking about, half naked?" asks Nick.

"*Briii-annn,*" Joe whines.

"Call you back, Nick," I say, and snap my cell shut. "What is it?"

"Something's wrong with Superman," Joe says again. "He's acting funny."

"Funny how?"

Joe takes my hand and pulls. "Come look," he says.

I heave myself off the couch with a groan, brushing the Hostess cupcake crumbs off my jeans as I get up. I've eaten six of them. The pile of empty cellophane wrappers is a testament to my dedication to perfecting my method—biting around the edges of the chocolate cake part without exposing any of the cream filling until the very end. It's harder than it sounds.

Joe leads me into our room. He lets go of my hand and squats down beside the small metal cage in the corner. He is wearing a pair of holey red sweatpants and his Pee Wee League baseball jersey from the previous season. He's already a pretty good hitter, better than I was at his age.

"See?" says Joe.

"Move," I tell him, pushing him out of the way with my foot. He scoots over, and I sit down on the floor beside him and we both peer into the cage.

Superman is pressed into the corner, trembling. He's a *fancy*. White mice are called feeders. Those are for snakes. Fancies are colored mice, brown or tan or black, like Superman. Joe wanted to name him Blackie, but I talked him out of it.

"Why's he shaking like that?" asks Joe.

"I don't know," I say.

It was my mother's idea to buy a pet mouse for Joe. She thought if she did, maybe he'd stop bugging her about getting a dog. Not only did it not work, but now in addition to having to share a room with my little brother, I have to share a room with a stinking mouse. Literally stinking.

"What's that reek?" Nick asked the first time he came over after we got the mouse.

"I don't know, but it's foul, isn't it? We clean the cage, and two seconds later it stinks again."

"Google it," Nick told me.

We typed in "Why does my pet mouse reek?" and found a site called "Know Your Mouse." That's where we learned that the problem was Superman's feet. Apparently male mice have scent glands in the pads of their feet so that they can leave love trails for interested females to follow if they're feeling in the mood. Instinct was prevailing over common sense, and Superman was laying down his trail in the exercise wheel in his cage, each rotation sending horny mouse musk wafting up into the atmosphere. And here I thought he ran because he was bored.

My cell phone rings. It's Nick.

"Is she dead?" he says.

"Who?"

"The landlady."

"I can't talk now. I'm dealing with a sick mouse here. Call you later."

Normally Superman would run away if you put your hand in the cage, but when I open the little door and reach in, he doesn't move. I scoop him up and gently place him in his wheel, but he just sits there trembling. Joe whimpers.

"I want Mommy."

This is not good. I've already got plans for that

hundred bucks, and I know if my mom hears Joe crying, she'll get in the car and drive home. She's a total sucker for his tears, especially since Dad left. Joe cries a lot, and he wets the bed sometimes too. Leaky kid.

"Let's let Superman rest for a while," I tell Joe. "Maybe he's just tired. I'll read you a book or something, okay?"

Joe brightens.

"*The* book?" he says.

I know which book he means.

"How about *Curious George* instead?" I suggest.

Joe shakes his head. He wants me to read his baby book, the one my mother made for him when he was born.

"Aren't you tired of hearing that stuff yet?" I say. "It's so boring."

Joe's eyes start to fill.

"Fine. Go get it," I tell him.

We sit on the couch, and I read Joe's baby book to him even though it's so corny it hurts.

"'The moment we laid eyes on you, it was love

at first sight. Our little Joe. Sweet baby Joe. Daddy held you all night so Mommy could sleep. In the morning Grandma brought your big brother, Brian, to see you. At first he was scared to hold you, but pretty soon he was a pro. He even changed your poopy diaper.'"

Joe giggles. This is one of his favorite parts.

We wade through pages of Joe's milestones, each one punctuated with an exclamation point, sometimes two. "Today you turned over!" "Today you said your first word, *duck*!" "You know where your tongue and hair are now!" "You can wink!!"

Joe's heard it all a million times before, but he can't get enough.

"Read the part about my favorite foods," he demands.

I turn to the section called "Baby's Likes and Dislikes."

"'You like peaches and bananas and raisins, which you call ree-rees. You do NOT like olives. We let you taste one, and you made the cutest little face and then you spit it out right in Brian's lap.'"

Joe laughs his belly laugh, which is funny because he's so skinny he hasn't got a belly.

He makes me read "Baby's Games," "First Birthday," "Sweetest Moments." Between this junk and all those cupcakes, I'm starting to feel queasy.

"More," says Joe. "More, more, more."

"Here's a good one," I tell him. "'While you were sleeping tonight, Daddy told me he's in love with some bimbo named Brenda and doesn't want to be married to me anymore. I cried and threw a frying pan at his head.'"

Joe grabs the book away from me.

"It does not say that," he yells. "You made that up."

He's mad now and full-out crying. I can feel that hundred-dollar bill slipping through my fingers.

"Calm down, Jo-Jo," I tell him. "I was just kidding. Can't you take a joke?"

Joe gets up and puts the book back on the shelf. "I want juice," he says. "And Honey."

Honey is Joe's blanket. Or what's left of it. He's five, but he still sleeps with it every night. He sucks his thumb too, which is why his teeth are messed up.

"Every time you stick that thumb in your mouth, you're putting another buck in some ortho-dontist's pocket," my mother says.

I pour apple juice into Joe's favorite cup, the pink plastic one that got accidentally melted in the dishwasher. He calls it the weirdo cup. Joe goes and gets his blanket out from under his pillow and curls up with it on the couch.

"Did Mommy really throw a frying pan at Daddy?" he asks me later, when he's done with his juice. I take the empty cup from him.

"No. But they did fight a lot."

"I know," Joe says.

"No you don't. You were too little to remember."

"I feel like I remember," he says.

Joe lies down next to me, nestling into the couch cushions and pressing his bare feet up against my leg. I get a sudden flash of my father lying on his back on the living-room floor with his feet pressed against my chest. He takes hold of my hands and straightens his legs, lifting me up into the air like an airplane. "Flyin' Brian!" he laughs as I let go of his hands and balance on his feet with my arms outstretched like Superman.

"Careful!" calls my mother from the kitchen. "Precious cargo." And even though I can't see her face, I can tell from her voice that she's smiling.

Nick calls again.

"Can you talk yet?"

Joe's thumb is in his mouth and his eyes are closed. It's way past his bedtime.

"Yeah," I say.

"Okay, we've all got the same picture, right? So where's the naked landlady from? She's totally dressed."

"She's lying on her side, with her back to the camera," I say.

"So? You can't see anything."

"Maybe not from the camera's point of view. But how do you know her shirt's not unbuttoned in the front?"

"Is it?" says Nick.

"It is in my story."

"Wow," says Nick. "That's bold. What's the guy with the cigarette doing there?"

"We haven't gotten to that part yet."

"So get," says Nick.

In the house next door to where the little girl and her mother were living, a teenage boy opened his bedroom window and leaned out. He had a book of matches in his hand, planning to sneak a quick smoke. Looking down into the neighboring yard, he saw Mrs. Androtti stretched out in the lawn chair. His eyes widened as he dropped the matches and ran to find his phone.

"Come on, man, be there." He listened as the phone rang, once, twice, three times—

"City Morgue," Mike said when he finally picked up.

"It's Jack," said the boy breathlessly. "Ask me what I'm doing."

"Why should I?" Mike said.

"Just ask me. Don't be a jerk."

"Okay, fine. What are you doing?"

"I'm looking at Mrs. Androtti's boobs."

"In your dreams," Mike laughed.

"No, man. I swear, I'm looking at 'em right now."

"Where are you?" Mike asked, and Jack could tell he had his full attention.

"Up in my room."

"With Mrs. Androtti?"

"No, fool. She's out in her backyard."

"Naked?"

"Practically. Her shirt's unbuttoned all the way."

"She got big ones?" asked Mike.

"Big enough."

"Sweet, man. Does she know you're looking?"

"Yeah, right. Like she'd show me on purpose."

"Well, who's she showing them to, then?" Mike asked.

"Mr. Androtti."

"That guy's a douche. He used to stiff me at Christmas when I had my paper route."

"Brett's a douche too," Jack said.

Mike laughed. "Oh man, can you imagine the look on Brett Androtti's face if he knew we were discussing his mom's casabas?"

"Who's discussing? I'm staring right at 'em in the flesh."

"What's she doing now?" Mike asked.

"Nothing. She's lying there, and Mr. Androtti's sitting beside her smoking a cigarette."

"If I was married to Mrs. Androtti, I wouldn't be wasting time sitting around smoking cigarettes. I'd be nailing her every chance I got," Mike said. "She's a total MILF."

"A what?"

"MILF—Mother I'd Like to, you know, nail."

"Oh," said Jack. "Right."

"What are you going to do if they start

boinking?" Mike asked.

"What do you mean?"

"I mean are you going to watch?"

"I don't know. That might be kind of weird," said Jack.

Mike laughed. "Or kind of great. Hey, maybe I should come over. You're not making this up, are you?"

"No."

"Sweet."

"Wait a second," Jack said.

"What?"

"Oh, God."

"Come on, Jackie. Don't leave me hanging. What's happening? Are they doing it?"

"Oh, God, Mike," said Jack, and he sounded scared.

"What?"

"He's burning her."

"What do you mean, burning?"

"With his cigarette. He's putting it right on her skin and holding it there."

"Is she screaming?"

"No man," Jack whispered. *"She's not even moving."*

My little brother stirs next to me on the couch and opens his eyes.

"Why did you stop?" says Nick.

"I gotta put Joe to bed," I tell him. "I'll call you later and read you the rest."

"It's really good," says Nick.

"You think?"

I make Joe brush his teeth and pee, and then I stand behind him while he climbs up the ladder and crawls under his covers. We share a bunk bed because our room's too small for two real beds. My dad and Brenda have a much bigger place. Joe stays there sometimes on weekends, but not me. I don't want to be anywhere near them. Especially now that Brenda's pregnant. Mom cried so hard when she found out, I thought she was going to break in half. I haven't told anybody about it. Not even Nick.

"Check on me in a minute," Joe mumbles. Then he rolls over and passes out.

I turn off the overhead and switch on the little lamp on the dresser, but as I'm leaving I hear this weird sound. *Shht-shht-shht.* Like a broom sweeping, or a dead leaf blowing along the sidewalk. I stand still and wait for it to happen again. *Shht-shht*—it's coming from the corner.

The little lamp doesn't give off much light, but when I lean over and look in, I can see Superman dragging himself slowly along the edge of the cage. *Shht-shht-shht.*

Something's not right. I don't want to wake Joe, so instead of turning on the light again, I pick up the cage and carry it out into the living room.

I speed-dial Nick.

"It's the weirdest thing I ever saw," I say. "Like somebody blew him up."

"Blew up as in exploded?" says Nick.

"No, blew up like a balloon."

Superman's body is about three times its normal size. If it wasn't so freaky, it might be comical. His pointy face looks like a tiny mask stuck on the front of a black fur ball, like a puffer fish with whiskers and a long tail. The reason he's dragging himself is because his stomach is so distended, his feet no longer touch the ground. He has to roll over onto one side, like a listing ship, and push himself along the bottom of the cage—*shht-shht-shht*.

"Maybe it's gas," says Nick.

"Do mice get gas?"

"Hell if I know," says Nick. "Squeeze him and see if he toots."

He barely fits through the small wire door in the cage when I take him out. I hold him, tail end pointing away, close my eyes, and gently squeeze. Nothing happens.

"Now what?" I say.

"Got any Tums?" Nick asks.

I get the bottle out of the medicine cabinet.

"What flavor do you think?" I ask as I unscrew the cap and pull out the cotton stopper.

"Cheese," says Nick.

"Ha ha, very funny."

I take a green Tums and hold it under Superman's nose. To my surprise he starts to nibble on it.

"Is it working?" asks Nick.

"Not yet." I look at the bottle. "It says 'fast-acting relief,' but it doesn't say how fast."

We're both quiet for a minute, and then Nick asks, "Why does Mr. Androtti burn his wife with the cigarette? Is he making sure she's dead or something?"

"Maybe."

"Why doesn't he check for her pulse instead?"

"I don't know."

"What do you mean you don't know? You wrote it, didn't you?"

"Yeah, but it's made up. It's not like it really happened."

"Read me the rest," says Nick.

In the apartment over the garage a woman stood at the kitchen sink rinsing out a blue sponge. Her little girl was in the other room, standing at the window.

"Mommy?" the girl called.

The woman reached over and turned off the water.

"Brittany-Michelle, I swear to God I'm going to come out there and smack you if you don't stop bothering me. Can't you see I'm busy?"

"But that lady's shirt is falling off."

"What lady?"

"The one from yesterday with the key."

"Mrs. Androtti?"

"Uh-huh."

"What do you mean, her shirt is falling off?"

"Come and look."

"I can't. I've gotta wipe down all these cupboards before we can put anything in them. There's roaches."

"She's asleep."

"Who? Mrs. Androtti?"

"Uh-huh. There was a man with her before, but now he's gone."

The woman brushed a strand of hair out

Sarah Weeks

of her face with the back of her hand. "Yeah, well, looks like Mrs. Androtti and I have something in common then."

She reached over and turned the water back on.

I stop reading.

"What?" says Nick.

"Nothing. That's it. That's the end of the story."

"Are you kidding? That can't be the end of the story. You haven't told us why Mr. Androtti killed his wife yet."

"It doesn't matter why he killed her."

"Yes it does. Everybody's going to want to know."

"That's okay. Writers do that all the time—leave stuff up in the air."

"I hate when they do that."

"Sorry," I say.

"I'm telling you, man, it's not right," says Nick.

Superman's on the move again. *Shht-shht-shht.*

"I don't think those Tums are working," I

202

say. "Any other bright ideas?"

"Yeah. Work on a better ending for your story."

"Why don't you worry about your own story? What are you going to write about, anyway?" I ask.

"I don't know," says Nick. "It's going to be hard. Compared to cold-blooded murder and half-naked women, anything I come up with is going to seem pretty lame, you know?"

It's after midnight when we hang up. I do my chemistry lab while I watch Conan. Nick was right, it's a hard one, but I manage to get through it without calling for help. I study a little for a Spanish quiz and then take a long shower. As I'm getting out, my cell rings.

"City Morgue," I say, figuring it's Nick and he'll get the reference.

"Not funny."

It's my father calling from the hospital.

"Sorry to call so late," he says, "but I thought you'd want to know. You have a new little brother."

"Half-brother," I say.

"We've named him Harrison."

"Okay."

"Brenda's doing fine. Fourteen hours of labor, though. She had a pretty tough time."

I resist the urge to say *"Good."*

"Do me a favor. Let your mother know, will you?"

Oh, great, I think. *Thanks for letting me be the one to deliver the happy news.* I don't say anything.

"You okay?" my dad asks.

"Yeah. Just tired. Plus Superman is sick."

"Superman?"

"Joe's mouse."

"Oh, right, your mother's idea of a pet."

"Yeah, well anyway, he's sick. Really sick."

"I had a guinea pig once when I was a kid, and when it got sick, the vet told my mother to put it in a plastic bag and stick it in the freezer for five minutes."

"*Grandma* did that?" I say. I'm having a hard time wrapping my mind around it.

"Most humane thing you can do with a small animal. No point in letting it suffer."

"Right," I say.

"Anyway, I need to get back to Brenda," my dad tells me. "I just thought you'd want to know about the baby."

I hang up, finish drying off, and go check on Superman. I'm relieved to find that he's somewhat deflated, but he still looks bad. There's something foamy leaking from his mouth now. It's pretty clear he's not going to make it.

I have tried to stay up all night twice in my life. Once at a sleepover party on Nick's birthday and once on New Year's Eve. Both times I ended up feeling sick somewhere around three, gave in, and went to sleep. It's three o'clock now, but I'm wide-awake. I decide that no matter how long it takes, I'm going to stay up with Superman until it's over. There's nothing on TV but infomercials, so I pick up my notebook and read my story again. I like it, but I decide maybe Nick is right about the ending. I sit on the couch for a while thinking about all the reasons why a man might decide to murder his wife until I finally find the one that fits.

The woman waiting in the car was nervous. He had told her it wouldn't take long, but she'd been sitting out there for at least ten minutes. Feeling some movement, a tiny internal flutter, she placed her hand protectively over her swollen belly and continued to stare out the window. Finally, he came out from around the side of the house and cut across the yard. He had taken off his suit coat and carried it folded neatly over his left arm.

"Did anybody see you?" she asked anxiously, as the man tossed his jacket into the backseat and ducked into the car.

"No."

I call Nick and wake him up.

"What's the matter?" he says, all groggy.

I tell him I took his advice and I read him the new ending.

"How do you come up with this stuff?" he says.

"I don't know. I just make it up," I say. But I know that's a lie.

At five o'clock I'm sitting there thinking about what a dumb name Harrison is when Superman starts to squeak. At first I think maybe they're happy squeaks, and that he's making a miraculous recovery. But one look in the cage tells me that's not the case. Talk about an audible exhalation: With each breath Superman writhes and pushes out an agonized squeak. I finally have to cover my ears.

Narrow bands of grayish sunlight appear between the venetian blinds. Dawn, and Superman is still hanging on. I may not be the best brother in the world, but I know that I can't let Joe see this. I go and get a sandwich bag out of the drawer. My hands are shaking so bad, I almost drop him as I slip the mouse into the bag. It's a ziplock, so I press the seam and watch it turn from yellow and blue to green. I open the freezer and put the bag on top of a box of Weight Watchers ice cream sandwiches. On top of everything else, my mother thinks she's fat now. I close the door and set the kitchen timer for five minutes.

I lean my head against the freezer door, and out of nowhere I start to bawl my eyes out. I'm still bawling when the timer dings. I wipe my nose on my sleeve, open the door, and take the bag out. Superman is dead.

"Brian?"

Joe is standing in the doorway. I didn't hear him come down the ladder.

"Go back to bed," I tell him.

"Where's Superman?" he says. "The cage is gone."

"I have him," I say, and I quickly turn my back and take the stiff mouse out of the bag.

"Is he okay?" Joe asks.

"No, Jo-Jo. He's not okay. He's dead."

Joe starts to cry.

"Poor Superman," he says. "Where is he?"

"He's right here, Joe."

"I want to hold him."

Superman is half frozen, but Joe is insisting, so I carefully wrap him in a dishcloth, and Joe sits on the couch crying softly over his dead mouse. After a while he looks up at me and asks, "Why is Superman so cold?"

"That's what happens when you die," I say. "You get cold, but you don't feel it."

Joe hands me the mouse and goes into his room. When he comes back, he has Honey in his hand.

"I want to bury him in this."

"Oh no, Jo-Jo. You don't want to do that. You'll miss your Honey."

But Joe's mind is made up. He carefully unwraps the mouse and gently lays him on the tattered square of blanket.

"This will keep you warm," he says.

The sun is barely up as my little brother and I carry Superman down to Riverside Park to bury him. We dig a hole under a bush with my mother's wok spatula and lay the tiny bundle in it.

"He was a good mouse," says Joe solemnly.

I never even liked Superman, but I am overcome with sadness. Joe thinks we should sing something, but the only song we can think of that we both know is "Itsy Bitsy Spider." We sing it together. My voice cracks a couple of times and I almost lose it again. When we finish singing, I take Joe's hand, and together we walk back up West End Avenue to our apartment.

VIVIAN LEVY

Sarah Weeks is an award-winning author of many books for children. Her novel *So B. It* was an *LA Times* bestseller and was named an ALA Notable Book and a Top Ten Best Books for Young Adults. Her other novels include *Jumping the Scratch* and the popular Guy series. She is one of the founding members of A.R.T. (Authors Readers Theatre) and an adjunct faculty member in the prestigious writing program at the New School University. She lives in New York City with her two teenaged sons. You can visit her online at www.sarahweeks.com.

THE
MOTHERLESS
ONE

Gene Luen Yang

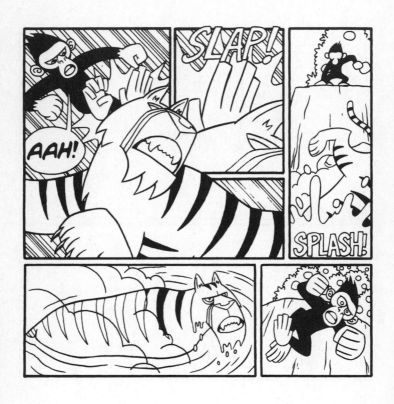

THERESA KIM YANG

Gene Luen Yang is the creator of the bestselling *American Born Chinese*, which won the Michael L. Printz Award and is the first graphic novel ever to be nominated for a National Book Award. He is also the creator of the graphic novels *Gordon Yamamoto and the King of the Geeks* and *Loyola Chin and the San Peligran Order*, as well as *The Rosary Comic Book*. When he's not writing and drawing, Gene teaches computer science at a Roman Catholic high school in California. You can visit him online at www.geneyang.com.